The Sleepy Hollow Incident

Book One

PD Alleva

Chamber Door Publishing, LLC

DISCLAIMER: This is a work of fiction. Unless otherwise indicated, all the names, characters, businesses, places, events and incidents in this book are either a product of the author's imagination or used in a fictitious manner. Any resemblance to actual persons, living or dead, or actual events is purely coincidental.

Chamber Door Publishing
Delray Beach, Fl

ISBN: Paperback: 979-8-218-82848-6
          Hardcover: 979-8-218-82849-3

Cover: Cherie Foxley
Editor: Chamber Door Publishing
Interior design: Chamber Door Publishing

Printed in the USA

For Dom, who always loved this story the most.

"You live your life, you go in shadows
You come apart and you'll go blind
Some kind of night into your darkness
Colors your eyes with what's not there.
~ Mazzy Star (*Fade Into You*)

Part I

Sleepy Hollow, NY

February 1997

1

The winter storm arrived with a vengeance and seemed to come out of nowhere. Sheets of snow blanketed a small parking lot as FBI Agent Henry Clavell parked his rented SUV. He had no business in Sleepy Hollow other than personal, but he'd been drawn into a situation that was beyond his understanding. He'd made the trek all the way from the Hamptons to the small riverside town of Sleepy Hollow. All to help a friend at the request of the mother.

He waited in his SUV, watching the red and blue lights troll across the shabby single-story motel. Why a woman with such a prominent background would choose to stay in what was clearly a trap house for local addicts was beyond his comprehension. It made no sense to him. Firefighters, policemen, and paramedics stood around the open motel room door. Most of them with startled expressions, lost in maddening thought over what they'd seen in the room with the door wide open. Captain Flannery appeared in the doorway, obviously staring in Henry's direction, waiting for him.

That's my cue!

Henry climbed out of his SUV, his heart hammering like a rabbit in his chest. When he first received the call from Flannery, he wished he'd never come to Sleepy Hollow. It's true that no good deed goes unpunished. True because here he was, in the middle of a murder scandal he was certain would become a new chapter in Sleepy Hollow's lore.

He locked eyes with Flannery, who waved him over before stepping back inside. From Henry's vantage point, he could see there was little light in the room. It looked like a deep black hole that he did not want to cross. But he knew he had to. He'd come this far and was so involved in the situation there was no possible method he could find to turn and go home and forget all about Sleepy Hollow. Forget Lori Francon, the reason he'd come in the first place.

Henry held his coat close to his throat as he walked to the room, snow pelting him in every direction. Noticed the awestruck stare in the eyes of the officer who stood outside the room. He looked like he'd seen a ghost, or he was about to puke. Henry always had difficulty deciphering the two.

It was dark inside the motel room, although not total darkness. Flannery had a small light set up in the corner that did its best to illuminate the gruesome scene.

"I got more lights coming," said Flannery, standing beside the bed, and staring at Henry.

Henry had no love for Captain Flannery. In fact, he understood the captain's skepticism about Henry's arrival, considering the string of bodies that blanketed his town since Henry first walked into Sleepy Hollow. But that was just coincidence, although Henry knew how police officers' think. They don't believe in coincidence. Henry met Captain Flannery when he went to speak with the officer in charge of the case, Detective Stephen Carver, about his friend, Lori Francon. Unfortunately, Detective Carver hasn't been seen since yesterday, adding to the mounting pile of suspicions in Captain Flannery's brain.

Henry had no response. He was too preoccupied with taking in the scene. There was a body beneath the bed sheet. The sheet was stained with blood, but not just a bloodstain here and there and not one thick and round bloodstain resigned to one specific area. No. The sheet was stained with blood from what must be head to toe from the body beneath the sheet.

He wondered if it was Lori who was under there.

Flannery's cover-up of the body confirmed what Henry already knew. Flannery suspected Henry was responsible for the murder. *He wants to see my reaction when he pulls off the sheet.*

The storm howled outside the room, cold and menacing, and Henry's blood turned cold in his veins. He raised his eyes to Flannery's, who raised his eyes to the ceiling. Henry followed his gaze. His body twitched inward when he took in the sight above him.

The ceiling was painted red. Red with blood. And the blood was moving like a snake across the ceiling, slithering with thick crimson droplets that dripped to the floor.

"Now, how do you think that happened? It's like the blood is still alive," said Flannery, staring at Henry with that skeptical stare, so ready for the big reveal Henry was certain the man was excited. As if he'd caught whoever was responsible. Caught him because to Flannery the murdering son of a bitch who painted that ceiling red was standing in front of him. "But wait, there's more."

Flannery pulled off the sheet like a magician tosses off a curtain to reveal the magic behind it. Henry's jaw dropped.

The body was gutted from throat to navel and hollowed out. There was no blood in the body-it was all on the ceiling-and no organs, just an empty, wide-open body. Henry immediately turned away, grinding his jaw when he saw on the dresser across the room all the organs that were removed from the body lined up perfectly and neatly across the top. A pentagram stained the mirror above the dresser, written in blood. Henry noticed one of those blood droplets dripped from the ceiling to the liver sitting center stage.

"We haven't found the heart," said Flannery. "Maybe you can help us locate it."

Henry turned his stare to Flannery. He could give a shit about Flannery's skepticism. He didn't do this and that's all the truth he required. Henry said nothing in response. What could he say, anyway? It's better to have a lawyer present when he's questioned by Flannery. As we all know, anything you say can and *will* be used against you in a court of law, and we all know how twisting someone's words can lead to a conviction. He was an FBI agent, after all.

"Is this your girl?" asked Flannery. Henry could feel the captain's eyes burning a hole through him.

Henry had been so preoccupied staring at the hollowed-out body he hadn't yet looked at the face. The face that had been battered and beaten to a bloodied pulp destroying all recognizable features. The bones were crushed as if someone used a rock to bludgeon the corpse. The hair was short, cut just above the ears and stained red with blood. The eyes were missing. The body style was short too, and husky. Henry knew who it was, but it wasn't who Flannery thought it was.

He shook his head and said, "No," through a closing throat.

Flannery lifted a flashlight from his belt, clicked it on and shined the light towards Henry's feet. "Recognize that size six?"

Next to Henry's feet were footprints. Small, bloodied footprints and yes, Henry recognized the footprint. Ironically, he'd seen the same this afternoon.

"They led into the parking lot when we first arrived. Good luck for whoever they belong to, considering the storm buried them before we could follow where they went."

Henry looked at Flannery. "No," he said, moving his head from left to right.

"Lots of noes at the moment."

"Something like that," Henry said under his breath. He wasn't sure why he was lying. Quite obvious to him, the truth would see the light of day, but he had to. That was the only way he could find Lori before Flannery put all the pieces together, and considering the body's condition, he could always use the excuse that it was too mangled to recognize who it was.

"Take a moment, detective. Get a breath of fresh air. I'll speak to you in a minute."

Henry had no reply. He simply turned around and stepped outside into the snow. His head down, following the trail those size sixes made. There were two additional footprints outside the room, although the snow was falling fast to conceal them. They were pointed in one direction. His eyes roamed to the western woods surrounding the motel. So dark and quiet. Sassafras and oak trees swayed in the wind with their bare branches stretching like veins into the night sky to the heart of the crescent moon above. The woods creaked and moaned as if in mourning and a thick fog drifted between the trees. A squealing, chattering screech yelped across the woods and sent a shudder through his bones. He scanned across the woods, hoping to see a light or movement in the moonlight that would tell him where Lori had gone. That was her size six.

And the woman lying dead in the room was her mother.

2

Lori kept hearing voices.

Or was it the wind howling through the trees in the western woods? When she first started her trek into the woods, the fog drifted between the trees and seemed to call to her, begging her to enter. The moon was prominent in the night sky, as if the overcast sky that had blanketed Sleepy Hollow all day provided a reprieve for the moon to watch over the Hollow. But the moment she stepped into the woods, the first snowflake danced in front of her eyes. The trees creaked, bending to the wind, as if someone wrenched and wrung those tree trunks until all they could do was groan to the moon like the final gasp from the dead releases all of life's hardships. A chattering echo erupted across the trees, and Lori's heart jumped in her chest. Although, she refused to allow those sounds to deter her mission.

She paused to take a better look at what lay ahead. The last thing she wanted was to get lost in the woods. Legend has it they were haunted. Haunted by the souls who met their death in these woods over the centuries. But Lori knew differently, the woods were haunted by their own memory of the dead, as if it sought to raise them from the depth of the subconscious to release them forever, but with no power to do so, they walked through the woods, angry and willing others to join them.

The snow blanketed the scene, and Lori squinted to see as far as possible. Looking for direction, the light in the darkness that would confirm she was on the right path. She tucked her bare hands into the crook of her arms, standing, staring, searching.

Release meeeee! the wind whispered. *Reeelleaeaeaeasssssse Meeeeeee!*

She felt a hand brush across the nape of her neck, and she spun around to the ghost that rushed through her bones with a snap of its jaw. Her heart tensed, her bones constricted, and her breath caught in her throat. She turned on a dime, watching the apparition disappear into the woods.

Reeelleaeaeaeasssssse Meeeeeee!

The voice faded with the ghost. Her hand went to her chest when her heart jumped from the screech from high above. The great horned owl stretched its wings and hissed at Lori. Its stare held firmly in her direction. Its mouth was gaping, screeching, and hissing before lifting off the branch in the same direction as the ghost.

Lori swallowed the breath that caught in her throat, watching the owl disappear into the snow. She took a step forward, then another, and kept moving.

I'm on the right path, she thought.

She was hoping she'd see it soon. The light. The single flame that burned just for her, in the window where no light was allowed. The light she was told would be waiting.

Hallucinations. Mind control. Manipulation. That's how the demon worked. He made you feel like you lost your mind. An effort to create confusion in the minds of his victims. Confusion for Marc too. Marc was Lori's ex-fiancé and the reason she returned to Sleepy Hollow.

She came to reconcile. To understand why he wrote the letter that ended their relationship. She came to find him, because there was still love in her heart for the man she agreed to marry. Tragedy being the catalyst that robbed Lori of her happily ever after. She knew now that if it weren't for Marc, she'd be dead already. Which is why she was walking through the woods in the middle of a snowstorm in the middle of the night. Too many people have suffered for the love they shared. Even Lori's mother, although Lori concluded she'd gotten what she deserved. The rest were innocent. Their only mistake was bearing witness to the manifestation of a loving heart, recognizing beauty the moment it blossomed.

She had to get to Marc. She knew where he lived. The old house in the middle of the western woods. The house that was more than two hundred years old. Lori knew it was abandoned and neglected, much like Marc was when she saw him earlier. He looked so different, as if someone had claimed a permanent space in his brain and changed the way he looked.

So many changes have occurred over the last six months Lori couldn't put her finger on when the changes began. Was it before or after the accident? Or maybe the change had always been there, waiting to be discovered.

Her hands were freezing, the cold nipping at her skin. She could hardly feel her face it was so cold, and the moon cast shadows across the trees that Lori was certain were waiting for her, watching the trek, knowing her presence was required. She took a step up a small incline and low and behold, the light was there. So faint and subtle. The candle burned in the window. Burning in the window of Marc's dilapidated house but so far off in the distance, her heart tensed in her chest. Other than the candle, the house was dark, foreboding, cast in the moonlight where the snow seemed to disappear. It seemed to call to her, as if she was a requirement the house had yet to claim.

Good thing for Lori, the incline leveled out and she could trek through the woods on safer ground.

Reeelleaeaeaeassssssse Meeeeeee!

The apparition stood between the trees, watching her. Angry. Determined. Haunted.

"I am," she hollered with a whine in her voice.

She pulled the wool beanie over her ears and moved forward through the trees. All the while keeping her eyes on the light. Everything led up to this moment, and she needed to confront Marc. Confront Marc and his demon.

Because what would you do if someone sold their soul to save your life? Would you give them yours in return?

3

Six Months Prior

Brilliant and disturbed.

That was Lori's first impression of Marc. She fell in love at first sight. Plus, he was the polar opposite of the people Lori normally associated with. He was poor, poor but proud, living in a small two-bedroom apartment. The same apartment where he grew up and how or why he continued to live there was something Lori could never understand, considering the only lesson his mother ever taught him was that sometimes the people you love don't love you.

His mother died when he was fourteen. She slashed her wrists in the back bedroom. Marc's father was away on business-he was always away on business-when she opened a river of blood across her wrist. Lori could never imagine the fourteen-year-old Marc when he discovered his mother on that fateful morning. A thought she wished to not have inside her brain, but what she could never shake was his expression when he told her the story. So much pain at such an early age. Marc once told her how his mother would force him to wait in the car while she attended the many dive bars across Sleepy Hollow, drinking into the early morning hours and how sometimes she would forget he was there when she finally made her way home, sometimes with a man-not his father, of course-and sometimes so drunk Marc was surprised they even made it home.

Always a ghost, Marc had said. *As if I was invisible. No one, nothing.*

And Lori's heart sank deeper into love with him. She wanted to protect him, to allow him to understand what love truly was. Because if she could do that, the world would be a better place.

Marc's father was another story. All indications revealed he was a good man, although his employment seemed more important to him than his son and how anyone could live like that was beyond Lori's understanding. Marc's father passed away a few years ago, a few months before Lori met Marc in a tearoom off Broadway in Tarrytown, the small riverside town that used to share the same name as Sleepy Hollow. He died of a heart attack while attending church services early on a Sunday morning. Marc said the heart attack was unexpected. His father was in good health and the doctor who completed the autopsy indicated that it seemed his heart had taken a jolt, as if he had literally been scared to death.

Marc was twenty-five when Lori met him, Lori was a year older. But those tragedies brought Marc to love ferociously and to live passionately. He was a writer, making his living writing a small column for the Sleepy Hollow Gazette. The pay was meagre, but he loved what he did and considering the two-bedroom apartment was subjected to rent control, he was able to make proper financial decisions to stay in the apartment which his father had bequeathed to him after his passing. Plus, the view of the Tappan Zee Bridge that stretched its steel across the Hudson River was what Marc had told Lori were like old friends he could always confide in, because they listened when all everyone else wanted to do was hear themselves talk.

His dream was to write novels that would change the world. Someday at least. And his writing was good. Really good. His words danced across the page and directly into the reader's heart.

Lori had moved to Sleepy Hollow six months after a horrible break up. She was glad she found that son of a bitch cheating. To Lori, he did her a favor, because she finally chose to leave her home in the Hamptons and get away from her mother, someone she could barely stand to be in the same room with for more than an hour. Pompous, opinionated, and manipulative was Lori's mother, Elena. The Francon family was always revered in high society social circles and when the family business was willed to people outside the family, Lori's father Claude was given an offer he couldn't refuse and relinquished all claims any lawyer with a brain would take on to get a piece of the family fortune. Instead, they took the money and ran. Good thing Claude's cousin Fredek had amassed wealth so abundant the Francon family name would be known for centuries and Claude made sure his deal was sweet. Unfortunately, he passed less than a year after cashing in, leaving Lori under the thumb of her mother. With no siblings to share the pain, and no distant relatives, Lori understood she was the last in what had been a long line of Francons'.

Lori rented an antique shop in Sleepy Hollow and moved into the top floor apartment without knowing a soul. If you want to forget the past, it's better to have no one to rehash it with, allowing those memories to wash away with the tide while you build new ones with your new life so you can be who you want to be and not the manifestation of the past. A month after she moved in, she met Marc in that tearoom. It started with a simple hello from Marc on his way out the door. He asked her if he'd met her before-an obvious pick-up line, but Lori didn't care. She couldn't take her eyes off his baby blues. They carried depths she wanted to discover for herself. Their meeting was short but profound and a month later, ironically, Marc made his way into Lori's antique shop.

He purchased a monstrosity of an armoire, and Lori agreed to help him move it to his apartment. I'm sure you don't need to know anymore, because this isn't a love story, it's a horror story, although all great horror stories begin the same, with an undying love that'll wrench the heart and squeeze until all the love is drained from the organ and all that's left is a hollowed out, withered and dying heart.

Time went on between them and Lori knew he wanted to tie the knot, as did Lori. She'd give up everything-Elena had informed Lori that should she marry Marc there would no longer be a seat at the table for Lori Francon Saduj, Marc's surname-and live in the two-bedroom apartment together forever. Living the simple life, peacefully and passionately. Lori had a feeling he was going to pop the question, and soon. When he informed Lori that he rented a cabin in the mountains for a weekend getaway, she was certain this was it. Certain that the weekend would live in the lore of their relationship for all their days. A time they would tell their grandkids about.

How right she was, but not the grandkids' part, because that hope was never meant to manifest. Nope, not at all. But the day will forever be ingrained in Lori's mind, not as the perfect day when she agreed to be his wife, but as the day when life changed on a dime and all of life's horrors came crashing down in a wallop across the head.

Sooner or later, we all must confront the past and the demon waiting in the forest of our mind, itching to be born.

4

It was a Saturday in late August. Lori woke up early to find Marc was already up, sitting outside with a five-subject notebook and a felt pen in his right hand, writing feverishly as he sat at a picnic table outside the cabin they'd rented. The weather was cool. The morning dew glistened across the hills and grass, but with a heat beneath the surface that Lori knew would take hold in a fever by midday. She fixed herself a cup of coffee from the pot Marc had made. Considering there was only one cup left, Lori knew Marc had been up for more than a few hours. He did that often, getting up way before the sun to write.

He entered a different world when he had that pen in his hand and his notebook out and Lori didn't want to interrupt him. Not that he would be angry with her by any means necessary, but when Marc was in that mindset, any conversation you had with him was null and void. According to Marc, it wasn't him answering or taking part in the conversation, but one of his characters. Marc considered himself a method writer and told Lori that once he was in the story, he was the character. Lori was grateful he never wrote horror novels.

She noticed the bottle of anisette on the kitchen counter, and she turned to the sliding glass door that led outside to the patio, watching Marc, his pen dancing across the page.

Lori stretched her eyelids, allowing some air into those gelatinous eyeballs-an attempt to shake the sleepy cobwebs from her brain-before she gripped the bottle of anisette.

"Guess we're starting early today," Lori said to herself, twisting the cap and adding a shot to her coffee. Stirred then opened the slider when a fresh wallop of damp air wrapped around her.

Marc hadn't noticed. He kept writing. He had a towel on the table that was moist with morning dew. His notebook was on the towel, and a cup of coffee next to the notebook. He loved writing with a simple pen and notebook. No computer required. When the time came to send the manuscript to publishers and agents, he'd type all those words onto a clean page with the typewriter his father bought him when he was twelve. She offered to buy him a desktop computer, but he refused.

"I don't know if I'd get used to it," he'd told her. "The creative process might take a hit with all that tap, tap, tapping of keys."

To which Lori gave a shrug followed by an "Okay then." However he wrote his books was no consequence to her.

Lori walked over to the table, and noticed there was no coffee in his cup, just a clear liquid. She guessed he had started really early this morning. She took a seat opposite him at the table. He continued to write feverishly. She took a sip, holding her mug in both hands, staring over the Adirondack Mountains bathed in greens and browns, rolling and sloping across the landscape. Crickets and birds sang songs as if to pay homage to mother nature.

It seemed like time stopped out here among the hills. Stopped to provide a moment where life's persistence came to a screeching halt, allowing the mind to process and release the anxieties of everyday living.

Marc's feverish writing stopped abruptly. Lori looked at him, his head down, staring at his short, dark hair. He always wore it short, his hair a Caesar cut that few men could pull off and still look good thanks to his tall yet thin body frame. At least, that's what the barber said. He sat there, with his pen in his right hand, hovering over his notebook. His left hand glided across the page. Obviously, he was reading what he wrote as a smile crept across his lips and he lifted his head, lifting those baby blues to Lori.

He cocked his eyebrows. "Now that was satisfying."

Lori laughed. "New book?"

Marc sat upright. "That it is."

Then silence as Marc gazed over the landscape. He was typically quiet after writing. He always said he needed to decompress. To rise from the abyss of creativity where he swam underwater for hours, finally releasing a thick, heavy breath when he resurfaced. Needed time to reassemble himself into the reality of mountains, terrain, streets, and people with beating hearts and blood in their veins and leave behind-until the next day at least when he'd dive right back into the fictional realm-the world that existed on the page.

They sat in silence for a while before Lori said, "So, what's on the agenda for today?"

Marc smiled as a glint ran across those baby blues. "Well," he said, gripping the handle on his mug. "I have a feeling it's going to be a great day. I figure we can go for a hike this afternoon. We have dinner reservations at seven and then…" He paused as if he hadn't thought past dinner. "Let's go for a walk around the lake. Sound good? Or we can go white water rafting instead of hiking. I'll leave that up to you."

Lori responded without a moment's pause. "White water rafting," she said. "Definitely." She finished her coffee.

"Sounds perfect. We should get ready then. Rafting in these parts is usually packed. The earlier we get going, the better. Plus, it'll give us more time before dinner to rest up." He flipped his notebook closed and Lori noticed the title on the front cover, written in red ink with thick letters. HOLER is what it read. Lori looked at it, perplexed, her brow knitted in confusion. Marc writes romance novels, and she thought the title was strange for a romance novel. Unless he crossed the line into erotica, but the word was spelled wrong. There should be two Ls. He clipped his pen to his shirt collar, then stood up, holding his notebook.

"I'm going to get ready. Been out here for a while and I feel all buggy. A shower is definitely required."

Lori stood up, too. "Me too," she said as a smile crossed her lips. "Maybe we can take that shower together?"

Marc offered his hand, and Lori took it. "My lady, I wouldn't have it any other way. Just think of the water we'll be saving."

To which Lori stated, "Depends on how long we'll be *in* the shower."

"Indeed," said Marc with a cock of his brow.

They went to the door and Marc slid the slider open. She stepped inside when Marc looked over his shoulder. She waited for him, dropping her mug on the kitchen counter. He seemed distracted, staring into oblivion.

"What is it?"

Marc looked left, then right, before turning around.

"Nothing. I thought I heard something."

She noticed he held his notebook tight against his chest. She gestured to the bathroom and Marc followed when she asked, "So, what's the new book about? What ladies are you romancing now?"

"None," he said. "This is a horror book."

5

The state psychiatric ward was buzzing with the crazies. Something got into them, some demon, and they were all howling and crying and screeching and clawing at their skin.

It turned the hospital into a literal nut house. Behavioral health technicians scurried frantically, attempting to secure every patient. They already used four-point restraints on four patients and there were no more on the ward. Instead, they insisted on physically restraining every patient while the nurse jabbed their arms with Thorazine. It seemed like something out of a horror novel.

Some patients ran into walls. Some lashed out, attempting to bloody those poor technicians. Every single one of the thirty patients had lost their fucking minds.

Dr. Lester received word of the uprising while eating his lunch-tuna fish- and immediately left that sandwich on his desk before taking the elevator to the basement ward. He knew what it was. That damn Wren was up to his old tricks again, whispering to the crazies and driving them into a frenzy. He did that every once in a blue moon, and considering there was a blue moon on the rise tonight, Lester wasn't surprised.

Wren was a lifelong resident at the state hospital in New York. He'd been there since his twenty-seventh birthday after he was found not guilty by reason of insanity for the murder of three teenagers in 1982. Although Wren presented coherent and sane during his trial, sometimes insanity can bleed over into sophistication. Think *Hannibal Lecter* for Pete's sake.

Wren had above average intelligence, coupled with an uncanny desire to eat human hearts. He once stated that the consumption of the organ brought the person's essence into the fold of his being. His words, not mine. He also stated that he was capturing souls for the master, though he would never say who this master was, other than offering a few biblical references that made absolutely no sense. He reported he'd been to hell and damnation, which is where his taste for human hearts originated. Said he'd travelled there after he stared into the eyes of a demon when he was twelve years old. He also said the demon groomed him during his time in foster care. That statement alone was exploited by Wren's defense attorney.

"He thinks he comes from hell. What else do you need to recognize this man is insane?"

Wren's testimony was enough to convince even the DA that Wren was clinically insane. Instead of the embarrassment of an acquittal, the DA offered life in the state hospital. Let them figure out when he was safe to return to society. Dr. Lester assured him that Wren never would. Lester had a personal interest in the case. One of Wren's victims was a girl Lester's daughter went to high school with. He promised to never allow Wren to see the city streets ever again. Once a murdering son of a bitch, always a murdering son of a bitch, and Lester wasn't about to sign on the dotted line and stake his reputation that Wren would never murder again.

Wren had been a ward of the state ever since, and that's exactly where Lester wanted him. Not that Wren could care. He seemed comfortable on the ward, as if he'd come home, although Lester was convinced that Wren was waiting for something. Some unknown time in the future when he could stretch his wings and rekindle his murdering impulse. If patience was a virtue, that murdering son of a bitch Wren was the most virtuous fucker who ever walked the earth. Although his confinement didn't come with a happy ending. Wren may have been incarcerated and locked away in a basement, but his murdering itch was satisfied on rare occasions.

Lester suspected Wren had played a central role in at least six suicides since his admission and more than a few cracked skulls. Always whispering was Wren. At least, that's what Lester's patients would tell him. They could hear Wren whispering in the wee hours of darkness, and it drove them into a frenzy. The recipient of said cracked skulls being the orderlies every time they got a little too close. Now Lester's ward was turned into a madhouse and the last thing he needed was another replay from the summer of '91. Not a chance. He lost three residents that day, four orderlies and two nurses.

He rolled his tongue inside his cheek, watching the elevator tick down to the basement.

"Give the whole fuckin ward a shot of Thorazine and shut em all up until tomorrow."

He looked up, grinding his jaw.

"Start with that son of a bitch."

He could hear the chaos before the doors opened. *Get ready.*

Once those doors opened, he was immediately assaulted by a patient who barreled into him with lightning speed. Lester fell backward, slamming into the elevator.

"He's waiting for you," screamed Clarice when she snatched his face in her hands, inching her nails into his flesh.

Yipping, screeching, and gawking rattled through the open door as Lester tried to pry Clarice's fingers from his face, but she kicked him in the balls and then wracked him across the head with a fist that should have felt like a fly she was so small but instead dropped him to the elevator floor. He looked up quickly, her talons about to claw into his eyes as the elevator doors started to close.

Jesus Christ, if that door closes, I could be locked in here with her.

But, as luck would have it, Desmond caught the door before it closed and wrapped his large arms around Clarice, snatching her in his grip. Thank God for good orderlies. Lester was certain he was about to meet Jesus himself. Clarice struggled in Desmond's arms, wriggling to free herself as Lester clawed to his feet.

"Four-point restraints immediately," Lester ordered.

"They're all done," hollered Desmond. "Nurses are giving out Thorazine shots." He shuffled with Clarice to the elevator door.

"It's a madhouse. Something's gotten into them. But only a few have been violent. The rest are all… all just nuts and howling."

Lester held the door open as Clarice screamed and jumped, attempting to free herself from Desmond's iron grip. "In her room then. I'll get the shot."

Desmond wrangled Clarice, trolling down the hall as she screamed and wailed, thrusting her head back, attempting to smash Desmond's nose into oblivion. Lester looked around the ward. Patients were in full bloom, pacing and rocking and running and howling, chattering, and screeching at the top of their lungs. Some climbed over furniture, and a few tossed pages from magazines and newspapers across the hall. Three patients were trying to wrench the television off the wall while others just sat and watched as if they were tuned in to a nightly show.

Lester made a beeline for the nurse's station, where he used his key to unlock the door. Betty Singer, a nurse who started a month ago, was filling syringes with a trembling hand.

"Keep loading up," said Lester. "We might as well have a quiet night."

Betty looked at him with panic-stricken eyes.

"Welcome to the nuthouse, Betty." Her only response was a dropped jaw. He grabbed the nearest filled syringe. "Send an orderly to Wren's room when you're done filling syringes. Hand them out to the nurses. One for each patient. Let's shut em all up."

"But sir, Wren is the only patient not acting out. We need…"

"Don't tell me what we need, Betty. Wren is the reason they're acting like this. Once we take him out of the picture, they'll calm down."

Now she looked at him like he was insane.

"Trust me," he said when a patient slammed into the door and Lester jumped while Betty dropped the syringe. Lester looked at her, then the ward, and all the crazies, although orderlies were close to non-existent. A few here and there, scattered about, grabbing patients in iron grips while the nurse provided the injection before the orderly wrangled the patient back to their room, only to return soon after. At least the patients weren't violent. Mostly just howling and throwing stuff or hurting themselves. Most of them, at least.

It's a distraction, he thought, thinking about Wren.

Lester turned to Betty. "Call a code red. All hands on deck. We're going to need reinforcements." She was hiding beside the desk, syringe now in hand, shaking, trembling. "Did you hear me?"

A tear rolled down her cheek, and she nodded as Lester reached towards her.

"I'll take that Betty. Just make the call and do me a favor when you get home tonight." He took the syringe.

"What's that?"

"Choose a different profession."

He dashed out of the room-forgetting to lock the door for poor Betty-and screamed, "Back to your rooms! All of you."

To which his patients all howled. Lester darted down the hall when one of his female patients raced out of her bedroom naked and screaming. She ran past Lester like he wasn't there.

"Simone," he yelled, but she kept running. Ran straight into the wall and fell backward, out cold and unconscious.

"Jesus…Christ, this is insane!"

And that's when old Fred walked by. Fred was a short and hefty old man who suffered from schizophrenia. He couldn't move too fast or scream too loud, so instead he cooed while throwing his hands up.

"Fred, get back to your room." But Fred kept walking and Lester shook his head. "Whatever." He opened the door to Clarice's room. Desmond was wrestling with her when he noticed Lester and slammed Clarice on the bed, holding her down with such force Clarice looked like she'd given up.

"He's waiting for you, doctor," said Clarice as Lester pushed the syringe into her arm.

"Take a nap Clarice." Lester stretched his back and stood tall, noticing Desmond was nursing a bloodied nose. "You okay?"

Desmond nodded. "She got me good."

"Well, no use crying over a bloodied nose. Betty is calling for reinforcements…" As if on cue Betty's voice crackled over the intercom calling for a code red to the psychiatric ward. "Need you to get back out there. Gather the other orderlies and nurses. Priority is any patient causing harm to themselves or others."

Desmond nodded, holding his hand over his nose. "Where are you going?"

"To the source of all this craziness."

"Wren?"

"You know it." And without a moment's pause, he scuttled out of the room into the hall and made a beeline for the padded party room, as he liked to call it. A few days ago, after they found Wren clawing at his skin, tearing off little tendrils of bloodied flesh, Lester ordered his confinement to the padded party room. He'd been draping the tendrils across the windowsill. It was a gruesome scene, but Lester wasn't concerned about Wren. He was in a straitjacket.

6

The shower was satisfying, quite satisfying indeed. The water had turned cold before they finished. So much for saving water. White water rafting was a host of laughs and scares. Lori slammed her shoulder into a boulder that Marc stitched up quite well, butterfly stitching the wound with the precision of a surgeon.

They celebrated with a host of ice-cold beers from the cooler they'd brought. Have alcohol will travel was Marc's motto. A necessary requirement for life's trials, tribulations, and celebrations. They drank and waited for the pain in Lori's shoulder to subside.

She took a moment to herself while Marc talked with one of the water-rafting employees. Marc was a classic case of both an introvert and an extrovert, depending on the situation. He was introverted when writing or at home, often preferring solitude, and battling his depression, which was a constant battle. Extroverted when required. He could change his demeanor on a dime if necessary and no one would be any wiser, never understanding how such a person could be so shy.

Most people put him on a pedestal, wishing they could charm a crowd the way he held them in his grasp, captivating their minds. Little did they know how he was with her, behind closed doors. How fragile and vulnerable he was, and how unsure of himself. There was a dark side to Marc that no one knew other than

Lori, fueled by a depression that could outlast any newfound success or gratitude.

But that was one of the things about Marc that Lori loved the most. His ability to step up his game when he needed to, never allowing his past to define who he is or was. Lori was intrigued about his new book. She wondered if he'd share some of it with her.

She sipped her cold brew, listening to Marc's high-pitched infectious laugh echo across the hills as he walked over to join Lori.

"Hey babe, this guy says we can go cliff jumping or take a tour of a cave. Are you up for it?"

He stood over Lori, blocking the sun, a fresh cold beer in his hand. He seemed like a shadow hanging over her. Lori looked up at him. "I think I've had more than my share of death-defying stunts today. Maybe tomorrow."

Marc squatted beside her, staring, as a smile curled across his lips. "As you wish," he said, his voice gentle, and Lori shared his smile, appreciating the sentiment. *As you wish* was a quote from their favorite movie. "How's the shoulder?" Marc used the cold beer and pressed it to the wound. "Numbing it up will help dull the pain. Does it hurt?"

Lori-eye's squinted from the sun-nodded. "Like a son of a bitch." She took a gulp from the beer in her hand.

Marc laughed. "I'm not surprised. You cut it open pretty good." He was looking over the wound, assessing his stitch job. "Do you want me to take you to the hospital for proper stitching? I'm not sure how long these will hold."

"No need. If we have to, we'll go tomorrow." Lori was a bit on the liquored-up side, choosing to not spend the next few hours in a hospital emergency room while receiving a lecture from the doctor about drinking and rafting. Plus, a hospital visit would put a damper on their plans for the evening.

"Ok. Let's stop at the store for some medical supplies so I can restitch it. We should probably change the bandage twice a day for a few days." He popped the tab off the beer he'd been holding against Lori's shoulder and handed it to her. "Take a fresh one." He took the empty can from her as she took the one he offered. "Ready to go?"

"After this beer," she said.

"Sounds good." He stood up, went to the garbage can and tossed Lori's beer into it, then took another cold one from the cooler and popped the tab open, taking a seat on a rock close to Lori.

She watched him as he did so, stretching his neck with a crack and pop before silence settled on their moment. They gazed over the hills with the sun high in the afternoon sky. Loose chatter, laughter, and rushing water filled the backdrop. Somewhere in the distance, the crickets were chirping. They sat in quiet solitude, drinking, staring, appreciating the moment as if they both meant to capture it and live there forever. But isn't it ironic how the moment we find peace the world seems to toss it on its head as a reminder that peace is something to be constantly fought for?

After a long while, their beers just about finished, Lori asked, "What time did you get up this morning? Seems like you got a lot of writing done, considering it's a new book and you filled up half of the notebook."

Marc paused before he answered. "Two o'clock."

Now Lori paused halfway through guzzling the last stretch of beer. "That's insane. How are you not tired?"

Marc cocked his head. "Guess I'm used to it. Three hours is plenty of sleep. I told you I was an insomniac growing up. Even now, since we met, I only get like four or five hours a night." He shrugged. "It's all good. Plus, I had a nightmare and woke up with a cold sweat and could have sworn someone was in the cabin with us."

To that statement Lori perked up. "What do you mean?"

"Well, I'm sure it was just the nightmare, but I could feel it, like someone was watching us sleep. Gave me the heebie-jeebies. I got chills and I couldn't shake the feeling, so I got up and went outside. Searched the cabin too, but there was nothing there."

"And then you started writing a horror novel."

"That I did. I got hit with the muse, Lori. And it's good. It's really good. I felt like I was in a trance all morning. Never even realized the sun came up, or that you came and sat down. You know how I get."

"That I do." She finished her beer and stood up. "Ready to go?"

"Of course." He guzzled his beer then tossed it in the garbage along with Lori's.

She watched him the entire time. He seemed to be crawling into his shell. She knew when it was happening. Like an energy she could feel churning in her mind, watching him slip away. Marc's ability to turn inward and allow reality to melt away like ice in the summer sun was uncanny. She knew he was thinking, thinking about the nightmare or the book or the presence he felt in the cabin.

Marc was plagued by nightmares. They were the reason he barely slept. Even the alcohol did little to numb the dreams. She watched him as he gathered the cooler, towels, and the beach bag Lori had brought, which he slung over his shoulder.

"You sure you got it all?" Lori asked.

"One hundred percent. Rest your shoulder. What we don't want is for it to rip open again."

To which Lori smiled. She hoped he would never change.

On the way to the car, Lori inquired about his nightmare. It took him a moment to answer as if he didn't want to say what it was or he was thinking it over, conjuring the nightmare from his memory.

"Marc?"

"Yeah. I'm here." Or maybe he drifted again. He did that often.

"The nightmare. What was it about?"

"Oh, that," Marc replied. "I got married."

Lori stopped in her tracks as Marc kept moving.

"To a frigin demon."

7

Lester pressed his nose to the glass window on the door of Wren's padded party room. Wren was standing in the center of the room, staring at the padded wall. No movement, no recognition. He stood there, standing, still and quiet, like a deer in headlights.

He was short, Wren was, and thin as a rail. Lester was a good six three compared to Wren's five feet six inches of skin and bones. His bald head gleamed under the light from above. Lester pictured his sunken beady eyes and large pointy nose. His pale, pasty skin and buck teeth and his large Adam's apple that looked like one of those hearts was permanently stuck in his gullet. Because of his appearance, and that he ate human hearts, the local papers coined Wren with the nickname Nosferatu. Plus, he enjoyed wearing black any time he was outside the psych ward.

Wren was always calm. Calm, cool, and calculated was the best way to describe Wren's demeanor. He just stood there, as if he were savoring the chaos and mayhem. Lester stretched his finger to the speaker on the wall to the left of the door and pushed the talk button.

"Wren," his voice crackled over the speaker in Wren's room. "Having fun Wren? Is this all because of you?" He waited for a response but received none, not even a head gesture to acknowledge his presence. "You've been whispering again, haven't you?" Lester moved his head from left to right and back again while clucking his tongue. "Not good Wren. Not good at all. I'm going to need you to drop to your knees and place your forehead on the floor, then cross your ankles, one over the other."

Before Lester completed his statement, Wren was already moving into position. One knee followed by the other, then he dipped his head to the floor and crossed his ankles. Howling from the psych ward erupted with a fever. Lester looked down the hall at the orderlies and nurses doing all they could to calm the patients down. Reinforcements had yet to arrive. Lester swallowed the breath down his gullet with a thick gulp. A bead of sweat dripped from his temple when an icy hand brushed across the nape of his neck. Lester's neck cringed, and he whipped his head around. Nothing. No one. He was alone in the hall filled with padded rooms.

When he looked back, Wren's face was in the window and Lester jumped back, startled and unnerved. "I said get down on the floor." Lester despised Wren's stare. He looked like a rat and Lester hated rats. Wren's stare was fixed, staring over Lester's shoulder. Not looking at him, his eyes lost in the space over his shoulder, and then Wren nodded as he closed his eyes. Then slowly-as if he were gliding-Wren removed himself from the window. Lester watched him glide to the center of the room.

"Fuckin guy is weird." Lester looked both ways down the hall. Other than the raging commotion, the hall was quiet. There were six padded rooms in the hall, and he knew three were occupied. Lester noticed the other patients were standing by the door windows, watching him. When he looked back Wren was in position. Lester unlocked the door, then gripped and twisted the doorknob, opening the heavy door wide against the wall. A musty smell greeted him as if the air had grown stale and required an exhale to release the negativity.

Lester was waiting for something. He didn't know what it was, but he sensed there was something coming he should brace himself for. He gripped the syringe tight between his fingers when he noticed his bones were all contracted and tense.

"Come in doctor," said Wren. His voice was a thick boom of strength and determination. He may be small in stature, but his voice carried the baritone of a giant, smooth and guttural. "So quiet in here, isn't it? I see you're having trouble with the depraved and demented. Should you need my assistance, all you have to do is ask and this can all be over so very soon."

Lester raised the syringe to his eyes. "Oh, it'll be over soon enough Wren, but without your help." He cautiously stepped into the room when he heard a deep inhale as if the room breathed him into it.

"Going to give me an injection, doctor? That seems like misdirection and abuse, considering I'm doing nothing but complying. I think I'll lodge a grievance with the state. See if I can get you fired."

Lester stepped over to Wren. "Don't move."

"Of course not, doctor. You've got to do what you feel is best, of course. I, on the other hand, must do what I am told."

Lester took a knee. "That's exactly right Wren. You need to do what I tell you to do."

"Oh, I wasn't referring to you, Dr. Lester, but if you need someone to stroke your fragile ego today, I am not the person to ask."

Lester gripped the back of Wren's head and injected the Thorazine into his neck. "There we go," he said, removing the needle. "You'll be out in a minute." He rose to his feet. "Might as well stay down there, Wren. You'll be out until tomorrow. Stop whispering to my patients or you'll be in this room for the rest of your days and that jacket will be your permanent outfit."

"Now that certainly must fit the definition of abuse, doctor. Do you treat all the sick and suffering like this or do you just have a hard on for me?"

"You wish Wren. Now go to sleep."

"Hmm," he said, "Or maybe it's that new nurse Betty you're saving that hard on for. I can understand why. She's quite the wild one once you get to know her." Lester's brow furrowed. "You should hear her thoughts at night. Quite the little vixen she is… but then again, it should come as no surprise. It's always the quiet ones now, isn't it?"

"Whatever Wren. I've grown tired of your antics."

"Trouble with Betty is that she gets so confused when she's startled. Seems she can't tell the difference between Thorazine and saline. I'll be honest with you doctor, I agree with your assessment. She should really do some hard thinking about a new profession."

Lester looked at the syringe when he heard a blood-curdling screech erupt in the hall and he snapped around with a startle. Clarice sprinted into the room and ran straight into him with the force of a freight train. Lester was tossed against the wall where the back of his head rapped against the padding, dropping the syringe in the process as he dropped onto his ass. He had only one second to open his eyes before Clarice was on top of him, sinking her talons into his eyeballs when the world went black and then the fists started coming, pounding across his face. His facial bones cracked and splintered as he slumped to the floor. Clarice was laughing while she bashed his face into oblivion. Lester drifted between dark consciousness and total darkness as Clarice started wailing, "What's up, doc? What's up, doc? What's up, doc?" pummeling his face into a bloodied gorge of blood and bone. His teeth cracked. His breathing turned hoarse, struggling, as if he were drowning and couldn't find the surface.

He heard Wren say, "Now, drive that syringe into his brain."

And he felt a pop in the center of his skull.

———

Wren was standing, watching the good doctor breathe his last gasping breath. He craned his head, staring at the bloodied pulp that used to be the good doctor's face. Clarice giggled with her hands cupped over her mouth. Lester looked so funny with the syringe planted in his skull.

"Now that was a long time coming," said Wren as Clarice turned to him. "I've been waiting almost two decades. Thank you, Clarice. Now, please unstrap me."

Clarice shuffled over to him, being sure to keep her head below his, and started unstrapping his jacket. "Have we done well, Wren? Will the master be pleased?"

"Indeed," Wren breathed. "He always honors loyalty. And you've been loyal for many years, Clarice. You have earned your rightful place in Xibalba."

She unlatched the last strap and Wren widened his arms, stretching his arms out of the jacket before hauling it over his head and dropping it to the floor. Clarice remained by his side, looking up at him like a lost puppy. He savored Lester's dead body before turning his attention to her.

He gripped her chin. "But there is one last trick he needs you to pull off before he escorts you into Xibalba. You've seen him, yes? In the halls and in your dreams?"

"Yes," she hissed. "His touch is like ecstasy. Turns my blood on fire."

"Indeed." Wren raised his chin, although his eyes never left hers. "The master requires his host and that right soon. I must prepare for his arrival. There is much to do. But first… first, Clarice, we need a distraction so I can make my way through the doors."

"Of course. Whatever is required. I am nothing but the master's humble servant." And she bowed. Bowed, and Wren placed his hand on her head.

"Good. So very good. But first, let us disrobe the good doctor. I will need his attire and ID badge if I am to walk out of here unharmed."

"And me," she said, her voice filled with desperation. "Me too, yes, Wren?"

"Oh, my child. I will see you in hell."

———

The nurses, orderlies, patients and supporting staff never saw the patient running at full speed and holding an oxygen tank. Never realized the elevator door opened and never saw the patient who dressed himself up like a doctor get on that elevator.

Clarice raised the tank over her head, running at full speed and screeching something awful. A scream that pierced their ears and brought their hands to their heads. Nor did they see their coworker Desmond lying dead in a pool of his own blood on the hallway floor.

There was one orderly who tried to stop it, but he was too far away to catch Clarice before she slammed the tank down across the concrete floor with the strength of ten men.

The last any of them ever saw was the fire that exploded from that tank.

8

"He was a nasty son of a bitch too," said Marc as he stepped out of the shower and grabbed a towel. Lori was brushing her teeth, a towel wrapped around her body, her skin glistening with beads of water. Her long dark hair wrapped in another towel.

She paused the brushing to respond, spitting a wad of toothpaste-filled phlegm into the sink. "Who are you talking about?"

"That demon guy from my dream. He was a nasty bastard."

"Why? What did he do?"

Marc dragged his towel across his body, drying himself from head to toe. "It wasn't what he did per se, but more like the energy in the dream. His energy. It felt like poison in my veins. Subjugation. As if I had to bend to his every whim and I kept hearing this loud gong in the distance, but..." He shook his head, then dropped the towel on the counter. "But it was also right on top of us. All I could hear was this gong sound, like a xylophone, but loud, really loud. It sent shudders through my bones. Through my heart too and my heart kept like... cringing or something. Like it was breaking or shattering into pieces. I felt hollow and alone. So alone." Lori noticed his eyes drifted, downtrodden, as if remembering the dream carried implications that could spiral the man into a new depression.

She wanted to reel him back in. "I thought you said you got married to him?"

Marc lifted his head, staring into Lori's eyes. "That's just the thing. It's like, in the dream, I knew we *were* married. Bonded with a single purpose. And he was in charge. I could feel his presence in my mind, suppressing every pure emotion and turning them into poison. And his eyes… all I could see were his eyes. Blood-red eyes as if he was born from fire."

He was gazing into the mirror now, his lost stare prominent in the reflection. That thin frame of his glistened in the mirror. Seemed like someone just walked over his grave. The longer he stared, the deeper he sank. Lori looked at herself in the mirror. Her nose carried the slightest slope to it. Freckles peppered her nose with just a few sprinkles across the slope. She turned her doe eyes to Marc. He's drifting again, she thought. She rinsed her toothbrush under the faucet and cleared her throat, snapping Marc out of whatever trance he was in. He offered her a smile before turning back to the mirror. He stretched his head towards it, studying his skin and his eyes.

Lori watched him from the corner of her eyes. "So, what did he look like?"

Marc, looking over his face in the mirror, turned to Lori briefly, then returned his gaze to the mirror, staring at himself. He leaned closer, staring into his own eyes. "He looked like me," he said, his tone soft and vulnerable.

Lori cleared her throat again, loud this time. She wanted him present, not drifting into the unknown recesses of his mind. It worked; he seemed to snap out of it. She took her blow dryer and makeup bag and went to leave but stopped abruptly and turned around.

"Did he have a name? This demon you married."

Marc nodded. "His name was Holer. Like ho-lair but not holler with two l's."

Lori remembered the title of his new book had the same name. Oddly, she felt a twinge of jealousy wriggle into her heart. She dismissed it immediately. "And where did this nightmare take place?"

"That was the even weirder part." Marc returned his gaze to the mirror. "We got married in Sleepy Hollow Cemetery."

9

Lori was still thinking about Marc's nightmare when they arrived at the restaurant. She had to check herself more than a few times. She couldn't believe she was jealous of a book and a dream. But she was also intrigued, wondering if the dream revealed a subconscious understanding of Marc's fear of marriage. Which made sense to Lori, considering his parents' marriage was composed of turmoil and heartache.

Perhaps he's afraid the marriage won't last?

And the demon is Marc's manifestation of that fear. Plus, since the demon looks like him, then perhaps-psychologically speaking-the fear he has is within himself. A fear that he could turn out like his mother and bring hell to the relationship. Hell to Lori too.

"Why are you so nervous?" Marc asked, taking her hand as she stepped out of the car. He was wearing his confidence; he seemed centered, grounded, as if he could shrug off all adversity. Larger than life, it was the Marc she fell for when she first met him.

"I wasn't aware that I was nervous."

Marc's head snapped back as if he was just hit with a wallop across his head, staring at Lori with a surprised stare. "You've been fidgety since we left the cabin. Haven't said a word either. Usually those are the telltale signs you've got something troubling on your mind." He paused for a moment, taking her in, assessing. "You sure you're okay?"

"Perfectly fine, actually." She noticed how quiet it was, as if the moon stole all the sounds from the earth and she felt a tightness in her gut, like an instinctive gesture to remind herself to be diligent and keep her wits in check. The air was sultry, casting beads of sweat across her forehead, her black cocktail dress clinging to her skin. "Just thinking is all." And she smiled, smiled to help ease the tension. Lori didn't know why she was nervous, but he was accurate in his assessment. Existing beneath the fold was something troubling. She couldn't shake the sensation that something was wrong.

Marc returned the gesture, his smile tightlipped, but his eyes sparkled. He closed the car door, and she looped her arm through his as they walked across the parking lot to the restaurant.

Lori didn't know why, but she wanted to wrap her arms around him and never let go. As if he was slipping from her grasp into some unknown void and she couldn't save him, couldn't hold on, and she wanted to grip him even closer, tighter, and bring him home and never let him out of her sight.

Walking into the restaurant was like walking into doom and gloom, a nervous vibration writhing through her bones. She couldn't shake it and desperately wanted the feeling to wane and be gone.

Marc was the picture-perfect example of calm. His confidence took center stage and helped ease Lori's tension. The restaurant was old and sophisticated. Crystal chandeliers hung in rows across the ceiling, reflecting the lights with glitter and sparkles. The tables were draped in white cloth and surrounded by high-back leather chairs. It looked more like a catering hall than a restaurant with a small dance floor at the far end and a small stage. A series of large bay windows covered the wall, providing a scenic view of the woods and the lake surrounding the restaurant.

They ate and drank and talked about the future, careers, and society. With the coming of the new millennium, the topic was a hot conversation ringing with fear and conspiracy over the unknown future. They talked about the dark veil, the theory that all we see is a simulation, spoon-fed through the media like mental baby food to keep us sedated and ignorant of what exists beneath the fold. Born into freedom with invisible shackles restraining all the power that exists within every one of us.

And of course, the fear that the world will end once the clock reaches zero to user in the new millennium.

"Consciousness," Marc said, "I think it has to do with conscious awareness. Of the self and society. A spiritual revolution in the midst of terror, depending on how far the mind has been whitewashed."

Lori paused cracking the crab shell in her hands. "Can you explain that in further detail, please?"

Marc paused too, holding his wineglass before he took a sip then placed the glass on the table. "Of course. It's a distraction. Too much information. All we see-magazines, movies, television, the news-is all designed to keep us looking away from ourselves. Always focused on the shiny object. We're like moths to the flame. Even religion, then toss in psychiatry. Here's a pill. It'll solve your problems. Here's religion. It'll solve your problems. Always reaching for an external solution to an internal problem when all the answers already live within. Now we've got this internet thing that everyone is indulging in. Information with the push of a button. But who controls the narrative? Who decides what information is fact or fiction? Eventually, it becomes too much information, and that's when we all tumble down a rabbit hole, seeking the very truth that exists within each and every one of us. But here's the rub, that rabbit hole never ends. Never comes to an abrupt stop, it just leads into new holes and spirals into new directions. All the while, the whole point is, you're doing exactly what they want us to do. Focus on the shiny object and pay no attention to the man behind the curtain. Little are we aware of the hell that exists beneath the shiny object, the real world. The subjugation brought on by the psychological shackle we all agreed to treat as though it is God. Sooner or later, we either wake up and embrace each other with a new lease on life, or we fall further down the rabbit hole, never able to see the light that exists within us. We should be accepting our individual differences. We should be conspiring for each other's success and celebrating each other's diversity, not at each other's throats and willing to destroy each other through some maniacal egomania." He paused and sat closer to the table as if what he was about to say was for Lori's ears only. "You see, we all have a power within us that they are afraid of. We can all overcome and move ourselves into freedom. This power exists within us. In every one of us. It lives in the heart and is fueled by our essence and our minds. So, while we're all looking externally to find the answers to fix ourselves, they sit up on high and laugh all the way to the bank. And then what? We're so distracted, all we do is climb into our metal coffins like zombies and mindlessly crawl across highways and byways to bleed ourselves dry for decades before we drop dead. And all for what? So that one day we might find the prize and break away from the complexities of the game they've set up for us?" He shook his head. "That's an illusion because the game never ends and most of the population has no chance of getting that prize without using force. They dangle the carrot in front of our eyes like dangling candy in front of a child, and it'll get worse. It always gets worse before it gets better, but that's just the point. If you want to destroy the psychological shackle, it'll take a lot of pain and that is where this conscious spiritual revolution will form. Out of the chaos those shackles have created. And if it doesn't happen. If they win their game, then one day we will all be imprisoned, made to walk in line according to what they deem is appropriate and all who step out of line will receive dire consequences. Complete subjugation. The last thing they want is for us to realize the game is bullshit and we can all choose, like that…" He snapped his fingers. "To wake up from it. When we realize we don't need shit from them is when things will change for the better. But that's how they keep us under the thumb. Making us believe that we can't live without them. Have enough strength to be yourself and stop looking at the shiny object as if it were a god." He paused and looked around, staring, assessing every patron in the restaurant. "It makes me sick to my stomach knowing how evil human beings can be. Most of them would sell their grandmother to get a piece of the pie and in the interim, we destroy each other and then chalk it up to some character defect or some other bullshit excuse that makes us feel better for taking advantage and destroying another human being. Look around you, Lori. These people are so brainwashed, sometimes I just want to pick up an axe and start hacking up every fucking one of them."

He was grinding his jaw, gritting his teeth and he had that nasty look in his eyes that turned Lori's blood cold.

"Or maybe just hold em and hug em and show them the light that already exists within. Maybe then the world would be a better place." He took a sip of wine.

Lori sat dumbfounded, her jaw hanging loose.

"Only love can slay the demon," he said. More like whispered, as if to himself. He set his wineglass down. "I think I've had too much to drink." And he laughed. Lori did too.

"People are always talking about *they*." She shook her head. "Who are *they*? Some mystical group of people pulling the strings?"

To which Marc responded, "Well, that's easy. Just follow the money all the way to the top and you'll find out who *they* are. They own everything and they own us, too. Why do we all go to work? Unless you're working for yourself, you're working for a company that they own so you can buy shit you don't need that is made by them while living in an apartment or house that is owned by them because they are the bank that loaned you the money so until you pay that fucker off it's all theirs. Driving around in cars we all paid way too much money for so we can feel better about ourselves and fool ourselves that we are getting ahead in life but all the while the bank owns the car until you pay it off and even when you do its worth shit by the time you've paid out of your ass for that damn car. They own all the media too, so whatever narrative they want to spin, they'll shove it down our fuckin gullet until we all choke on it." He slammed his fist on the table. Hard too. The cutlery, glasses and plates shook violently and more than a few patrons turned in their direction. "Makes me sick to my fucking stomach."

Lori shook her head. "Sorry I asked."

Marc snapped his head to her, his eyes beady and glassy. Lori stuck out her tongue and blew a fart across her lips that turned Marc's hateful gaze into a laugh. "That's why I love you, babe. You always know how to make light of any conversation."

The lights flickered in the restaurant with a buzzing beneath the fold.

"What *is* that?" Marc said, staring at the ceiling the same as every patron in the restaurant.

Lori looked at Marc. The light continued to flicker, casting competing shades of dark and light across the table. Across Marc, his features seemed to change with that light to dark flicker. Under the light, he was Marc. Dark hair, blue eyed Marc with that half-cocked Elvis smile Lori couldn't get enough of. But when the lights turned off, he looked different. His eyes were blood red, his lips thin and cocked back in a sneer. Normally his face was round where now it was long and thin. His nose in the dark was pointy where under the light it was small and round. But it was those red eyes that captured Lori's attention. Eyes that carried blood in them, staring at Lori with intent, as if those eyes could devour every fiber of her being and tear her soul apart.

Now the lights remained off, bathing the restaurant in darkness. A few hushed gasps and choked back stutters were heard in the backdrop. She couldn't see more than a few inches in front of her face. Except the eyes. Those blood-red eyes continued to stare. Intent. Angry. Hateful. Seemed like everyone lost their voice. Seemed like time had stopped. Waiting for the light to return to set the wheels of time back into motion.

Lori couldn't move. Her heart tensed as if the organ lost the ability to beat and thump. Held breath. Silence. Quiet. The eyes. Those red-beaming eyes filled with hate. All she could see were those eyes. No face. No nose or mouth. No cheeks or forehead. Just two red eyes in the darkness like stains on a black canvas.

She prayed for the light to return as fear rose in her chest. She couldn't breathe, her lungs constricted as if the absence of air turned those lungs into shriveled corpses. Panic. Her bones tense as if in protest over the lack of oxygen. And then those red eyes spoke.

Not directly, but she knew the voice in her head belonged to those eyes.

"Your death is required, my lady. And your resurrection. Your spells cannot save you."

Lori's mouth fell open as a choked back stuttered whine released from her throat.

"Tell me Lori, when the time comes, will you have the strength to destroy what matters most to you?"

Now there came a screech and a hiss. Lori stared through those red eyes, looking past them to the owl outside the bay window, screeching with its wings erect as a shudder erupted through Lori's body, rippling from her neck to the base of her spine.

Lori?

The owl's mouth was wide open, hissing and screeching. Its eyes were menacing, staring through Lori as if it meant to tear her heart in two.

"Lori? Lori, please."

The owl stretched its wings then lifted off the branch towards the window. Lori cringed and moved back.

"C'mon babe. Breathe, girl. Just breathe."

The owl thrust its talons towards the window that cracked and splintered, then popped with a crash to the floor when the owl swooped through the open window. Its talons stretched towards Lori, as if the owl meant to tear her eyes from her skull. She backed up. Backed up and tossed her arm over her eyes before falling off the chair, landing on the floor with a thud. She looked up quickly, and the owl was there. The talons nipped into her eyelids. The wings batting across her head.

She screamed from the top of her lungs when the talons sank into her eyeballs. Searing white-hot pain rifled into her brain as those talons squeezed. She fought against the wings, moving back and forth to get this fuckin owl off her. Felt those talons tear her eyes out and lift off her body. Saw herself with no eyes in her skull, writhing and screaming. Screaming so loud the heavens wept.

"Lori, babe. Open your eyes."

Marc's voice seemed far away, as if his words were enveloped in cotton. She kept screaming and flailing. The pain in her head was immense, and she felt blood gush across her skin.

Marc hollered, "Looorrrrriiiiiiiiiiiii," and slapped his hands in front of her face.

Lori jumped out of the waking nightmare. Lying on the floor of the restaurant. She saw the light overhead beam into her eyes. Marc was beside her, kneeling, his hand on her cheek, the other behind her head. Her heavy breath huffing from her lungs, her chest rising in unison with every breath.

"Calm down, babe. Calm." Marc breathed slowly, coaching her to breathe. "It's okay," he said, "You're safe." He moved his head left, then right. "It's over, babe. Just breathe. Deep, slow, steady, breathing. Calm now. So much calmer." His hand was over her heart. Lori felt sweat across her skin. Her breathing dwindled into a calm, natural rhythm.

Lori pursed her lips and swallowed with a gasp. There were many patrons and staff standing behind Marc, looking down on her.

Marc touched her face. "You okay? Can you get up?"

She went to speak, her lips moving, but no words came. She closed her eyes, taking a moment's pause, a brief interlude to allow her thoughts to catch up to her mouth. "What happened?"

"You had one of your waking nightmares."

Lori turned her eyes away.

"Can you get up?"

Lori nodded and Marc helped her to her feet as a waiter brought her chair closer. "Thank you," Marc said. "Here, babe, sit down for a second."

Lori sat down, hunched over, elbows on her knees, her head in her hands.

Heard Marc say, "Thank you, gentlemen." He shook hands with one of them. "She suffers from night terrors." She was trembling, her stomach twisting like a knife turning over in her gut. "Happens from time to time. I think it had something to do with the lights." Lori wrapped her arms around her stomach and started rocking. Marc whispered in her ear, "Do you want to go?" To which Lori nodded feverishly.

"Okay," he said, "I'll get the check."

10

Lori suffered from night terrors for as long as she could remember. When she was a child, they surfaced a few times a week and she could remember intimately the rage she suffered from her parents during that time. It wasn't as if they were nasty sons of bitches by any means. They just had no idea what they were dealing with. Especially since she was awake when they happened, so they never thought it could be a waking nightmare. They'd never heard of such a concept.

But they were there, and in the beginning, the classic family cover-up was the first and most important aspect concerning what Lori's parents referred to as her *condition*. The incidents continued and after some time, Lori's parents agreed to take her to see someone. Said someone being a psychiatrist in another state because Lori's father knew every psychiatrist worth a damn in New York and that would have been all he needed: word of his daughter's insanity rippling through the New York grapevine. He'd have nothing to do with it and would have brought Lori to Europe if he had to.

Those blood-red eyes and the owl have been the main characters in Lori's night terrors since the beginning. The doctor said the condition was not a concern, nor was it a sign of deeper trouble. "It's just a fear reaction brought on by moving from one sleep stage to the next." The doctor had also said they would go away in time. He was right, too. Well, almost right, because the night terrors subsided but never completely vanished. Before this fateful night, the last night terror she'd had was the first night she slept in Marc's apartment.

Now, as she sat in the car with Marc driving, she remembered her terrors vividly. Always the red eyes, and always the owl clawing at her eyes. She couldn't shake those eyes from her memory. Typically, with a night terror, the visions faded when she surfaced into consciousness or after she went back to sleep and awakened the next day with no recollection of the night terror happening. But on nights like this, when the waking nightmare found her, she carried the vision of those eyes and the owl until she woke up the next morning and remembered vividly all the night terrors from the past. They all had the same red eyes.

"You okay, babe?" Marc looked over at her, then turned his eyes to the road. Both hands on the wheel, driving quietly along the winding road.

Lori felt like run over dog shit. Her skin was clammy and drawn. Her stomach was twisted into knots that refused to relent, and her hands were shaking. Her whole body was shaking. She rested her head against the headrest.

"Babe?" Marc said. He looked at her again, then turned his eyes to the road, and stretched his hand to hers, taking her hand with a gentle squeeze. "It'll be okay. It's over now."

She couldn't find her voice. Felt all numb inside. Petrified and embarrassed. He looked at her again and offered a gracious smile.

"It's okay," he said, "I love you. I won't let anything bad happen to you. I promise."

Now Lori smiled. She couldn't help the reaction-Marc was so sweet-but the smile faded quickly with the remembrance of those eyes. She closed her eyes and the eyes were there, waiting, watching from the dark void. Always watching. Those hateful, menacing eyes.

"What's wrong with me?" she whispered.

Marc turned to her, then quickly returned his gaze to the road. "There's nothing wrong with you. Every person on the planet has things they need to overcome. You're no different than everyone else. Plus, they don't happen all that often and like you said, they seem to fade over time, so maybe that is what is happening and one day they will be no more."

She pursed her lips and turned to the passenger window, watching the trees and hills troll across the landscape. "I hope so."

Marc shrugged as he turned into the driveway. "And if not, we will deal with them together."

Lori turned to him. "You're not embarrassed?"

Marc scoffed at the notion. "Not a chance. Fuck everyone anyway." The tires rolled across gravel and earth towards the cabin when Marc stopped the car. He unbuckled his seatbelt and turned to Lori. "I love you, Lori Francon. I'd walk through hell to keep you safe. Whatever we need to go through, we go through together. Forever and ever until the end of time."

"Is that what this is, Marc? Forever and ever until the end of time."

He clucked his tongue. "Absofuckinlutely."

To which Lori laughed, grateful for the ease in the tension in her bones. "Well, put your money where your mouth is. I've been waiting a long time."

"Oh pressure. Don't know if I can handle it."

"You better." And she laughed, laughed out loud because she knew what he was thinking.

Marc cleared his throat before he said, "We leave tomorrow. I'd like to go for a walk around the lake. You up for it?"

"Sure. A long, peaceful walk sounds perfect."

"Fantastic. I'll fix some drinks to take with us."

11

They went skinny-dipping. And why not? No one was even close to the lake. The moon glowed overhead, casting silvery light across the trees and the water that was so still and calm, Lori thought twice about disturbing the peace.

The air carried an elusive vibration like an uncertainty that thickened upon arrival to conscious awareness. In fact, Lori had a sneaking suspicion they were being watched. As if all the creatures in the forest arrived to witness the moment of lovers with hope for the future, all the while knowing the tragedies that exist across the timeline of life were about to come crashing down without sympathy or remorse.

Lori watched as Marc swam towards her. He seemed nervous, like he wanted to say something but couldn't connect the words from his brain to his lips. His breathing was shallow as he trudged towards her.

"It's so quiet," Marc said, stretching his arms in the water, coming closer.

"It's after midnight. I'm sure everyone on this lake is sleeping."

Marc swam around her, nudged her in the back and kept circling until they were face to face. His stare cut through her, that unknowing nervous stare filled with adoration and uncertainty.

And then he smiled and came closer, wrapping her in his arms. Nose to nose, he stared into her eyes.

"I love you," he said, and Lori smiled. "You know that, right?"

"How could I not? You tell me all the time. But do you know I love you too?"

Now Marc smiled. "Without a doubt." He dipped his forehead to hers, their breathing soft yet profound and she could feel his heart beating he was so close to her, and then he kissed her. Soft, passionately, his hand over her cheek, his other arm around her waist. Kissed her and then touched his forehead to hers, taking her hand in his and spinning them around in the water, casting soft ripples across the surface. Lori noticed goosebumps across his skin. The water was so cold, Lori trembled in his arms. She leaned her head against his shoulder, and he wrapped his arms around her, holding her tight.

"Cold?" Marc asked.

"Freezing." Lori tightened her grip around his shoulders and Marc kissed her neck, her cheek and then her lips. Soft, open mouth with a kiss that confirmed his desire. She felt love in that kiss, everlasting love that would stand the test of time. His breath hot and stuttering, hers too. Their noses close, so close. He kissed her again, long and filled with passion, then lifted her hips close to his, parting his lips from hers. Lori's eyes opened, staring into his eyes, so nervous and uncertain. And then he smiled.

Smiled and said, "Let's see if we can warm you up."

And he kissed her again. They made love in that lake that night. Made love and when they returned to land, Marc wrapped them in the comforter he'd brought. He asked her to be his wife by that lake. Asked her to spend a lifetime with him, to be his bride, his partner, his everything. And Lori graciously and feverishly accepted.

Little did she know it was the answer that would seal their doom. Little did she know there was a demon waiting in the woods.

12

"Storms coming," Marc said. "We should try to beat it out. Looks like it's coming from the north."

Lori was walking through the cabin, making sure they left nothing behind. Marc had finished packing the car and was eager to leave. "Ok. I'll be done in a minute."

Marc smiled, staring at her. She knew how proud he was, ready to spend the rest of his life with her. "Okay. I'll be in the car." He flipped the key ring around his finger then stepped out of the cabin. Lori watched him as he looked up at the sky where a distant black cloud was creeping slowly towards them.

She returned to the task at hand. When Lori was a child, she left her favorite stuffed animal-an owl, ironically-in a hotel room where she was staying with her parents. The loss directly resulted in Lori's need to search every inch of whatever hotel room or cabin she stayed in for the rest of her days. She searched the bathroom, the kitchen, opening all the cabinets and drawers. Found a few hair ties in the bathroom drawer and stuffed them into her pocket. Looked through the bedroom closet too, but there was nothing to be found. Satisfied, she went to leave when she glimpsed something blue in the corner of her eye. She turned to the bed. The comforter draped over the mattress hovered an inch above the floor, but she could see it. Something was under the bed and when she flipped the comforter over the mattress, she was surprised to find Marc's new book, the blue five-subject notebook he'd been writing in, beneath the bed. The title 'HOLER' written in red ink across the front.

How could he have forgotten his book?

Lori shook her head as she stood up then walked through the cabin, scanning across it in case a little trinket was left behind. There were none, and she walked through the front door into the dark of the storm. A warm breeze greeted her the moment she stepped outside. Marc was in the driver's seat, but she couldn't take her eyes off the rolling dark clouds that seemed to devour all in its path.

Marc tapped the roof of the car. "Ready to go?"

She gripped his notebook tight against her chest and went to the car. "You forgot your book," she said, handing it to him before she took her seat.

Marc was quiet, looking over his notebook, confused. "Where was it? I thought I packed it."

"Maybe it fell out, and you didn't notice." She was preoccupied with staring at the sky and the coming storm.

After a minute, Marc whispered, "I guess so," then turned and wedged the book between the seat and his duffel bag in the back. "Ready to go?"

"Ready as ever."

He put the car in reverse. "Got a long drive ahead. Hopefully, we beat this storm. It looks like a nasty fucker."

13

She was dreaming when the storm hit full force. Dreaming of the red eyes.

Red eyes following them down the highway. Up above the trees, in the sky filled with dark clouds. Red blazing light etched into the sky. In the dream, everywhere she looked, she saw red light, as if the coming storm sliced into the heart of the heavens and spilled blood over the horizon. She wasn't in the car anymore. In the dream, she was walking through the woods, searching. For what, she was never certain, but she knew she had to keep searching, wandering through the woods, helpless. And every time she saw the end to her journey she had to begin again. Circling in an endless loop with that blood red sky descending upon her.

Do you know what it is like to be frightened?

To be scared to death of the shadow in the corner?

She was running now, running to the end of the woods as the voice echoed across the heavens.

Allow me to show you what fear looks like.

Allow me to reveal the depths of the human heart.

Now she could hear a heart beating. Hers or the voice's heart she wasn't certain, as she ran, ran through the woods with the hope she could escape. Up ahead and just out of reach was the clearing where she understood she would find freedom. Her breath caught in her throat. Her heart groaned to be free.

And standing in the clearing was Marc, looking away into the distance. Perhaps at the blood red sky. But he looked different or felt different. Something was wrong. Something was very, very wrong with Marc. Lori stopped cold in her tracks. It looked like he was talking to someone, his voice so soft she thought he was whispering. And then he laughed. Laughed out loud and Lori stepped closer, nearing the end of the woods.

What she had first thought was green and healthy foliage was withered and decayed. Grass as brown as asphalt, trees bent and dying with bare branches that groaned as if the wind caused them pain. She looked around, to be sure it was safe, wondering who Marc was talking to.

She stepped closer. Her foot snapped a branch and Marc fell silent. His body language stiff. She took another step and noticed the man beside Marc. Tall and lanky, and wearing all black. Shirt, jacket, pants, and boots. His hair, thick and long, cascaded to his shoulders. His face was thin, with skin turned grey with black blotches as if the skin was decomposing. But it was his eyes that captured Lori's attention. Blood-red eyes stared at Lori, and then he laughed. Marc did too, and it was then that Lori noticed Marc's eyes were the same blood red.

"Get away from him," Lori grunted, her teeth grinding. But they continued to laugh, to laugh out loud. "I said *get away from him!*"

And with that, the laughing ceased. Their expressions turned confused. At least for Marc, but the demon standing next to him seemed to cringe at her words, his stare driving a stake through her heart.

"No Lori," he called to her. "There's only one way this all ends." And he stepped behind Marc, who jumped with a startle when he put his hands on his shoulders. "Turn, boy. Let her see how feeble you really are." He turned Marc around and pushed him forward a few steps. Marc held his head down. He seemed to shrivel in Lori's presence. Lori noticed her hands were trembling. Her lips too, her head moving back and forth.

"No," she said, "Get away from him."

"Oh, Lori." The demon craned his head, glaring at her. "You want his heart?" He stepped closer to Marc. "Very well then…" He paused, and Lori could see Marc's eyes carried desperation and fear. "Take IT!" And the demon punched through Marc's spine, his shoulders hunched back as the demon's hand ripped through his chest.

In his hand, he held Marc's heart. She could see it was still beating, and all she could hear was screaming as Marc looked down at the heart in the demon's hand. Screaming so loud she never realized the scream was coming from her own throat. Marc lifted his eyes to her.

"You have to, Lori," Marc said, his voice defeated and broken, garbled with blood. "It's the only way." He slumped to his knees as the wind rifled into a frenzy and all Lori could see was the demon, standing, laughing, devouring Lori with his eyes as he kicked Marc's body to the ground and held the heart high for Lori to see. "Come Lori," he said. "Come and find me."

And he bit into the heart when Lori darted out of the woods, running. Running towards the demon and screaming. Screaming all bloody hell when she jumped and found herself in the car. Marc was driving. Darkness surrounded them. The storm was in full effect. Raindrops pelted the windshield in sheets.

"Holy shit, are you okay?"

Her heart was racing in her chest, her breath constricted. Gasping. Huffing. Hard to breathe. Sweat as thick as bullets dripped off her brow.

"What the hell just happened?"

She was hyperventilating. Her mouth wide open, her chest tight as if refusing to allow air into her lungs. Felt like choking. Panic! Everything was tight, airless, as if the air was sucked out of the car and she was gagging, her eyes popping out of her skull.

"Jesus Christ!" Marc looked at her quickly, then turned back to the road. "Lori!"

She was pinned to the seat, desperate to bring air into her lungs. Marc looked at her and the car swerved across the road into oncoming traffic. Headlights and horns, and Marc swerved back into his lane. Lori felt that wave of panic return tenfold when the car careened around the corner, skidding. They were still in the mountains and Lori thought they were going to skid off the side and tumble to their death.

Slow motion, she saw Marc with panic in his eyes, grip the steering wheel tight, attempting to take back control when her eyes darted to the black sky and the red eyes that speared towards them with a crack of lightning on the heels of thunder.

"What the fuck!"

That was Marc's voice. The last she heard before the car veered off the highway and clipped a tree. Then tumbling. The car was tumbling over and over, finally skidding across the asphalt to a stop.

The smell of smoke, gas, burning rubber, and oil. The sound of rain pelting the car. A scream like a siren going off in her head.

Lori slipped into the unknown.

Part II

14

Killing isn't hard to do. All it takes is determination and will.

Marc awakened with a sudden jolt and a gasp. White, bright, and shiny washed into his vision. His chest heaved, drawing in a deep breath as the sound of bleep, bleep, bleep rang through the room. And then the pain arrived with vengeance. The left side of his vision was blinded, his head throbbed, his eyes were on fire, and his ribs twisted pain into his skull when he moved. Wires, no, tubes cut into his left arm and that bleep, bleep, bleep kicked into overdrive.

Having a conscience matters not. That's just a part of the consequence.

Panic. His one eye stretched wide, wrenched open by the lack of oxygen to his lungs.

But any person can toss off consequence with a shrug.

You, too, can do the same. All in time.

All in time, indeed.

As if on cue, a nurse rushed into the room.

Marc jumped, startled. Jumped to get and go and run, when he noticed his arms were strapped to the bedrail.

"Calm down Mr. Saduj," the nurse said, her voice pressured. "Just breathe. Calm and slow." She placed her hand on his chest, coaching him to breathe.

He felt his breath begin to calm, staring at the nurse, confused and disoriented.

"Good," she said. "Stay calm." She breathed with him, slow steady inhales followed by long, relaxing exhales. "You've been combative since you arrived. I don't want to sedate you again. Try to stay calm."

Beyond the nurse, sitting in the corner, was a man dressed in all black. He had long dark hair that hung in tendrils to his shoulders and his skin was gray with black blotches that made him look like he was decomposing. He was holding a red cane that he continuously kneaded into the tile floor. The man in black looked at Marc and smiled a thin, toothless grin. Marc's throat hurt something awful, and when he went to speak, to ask why the man in black was sitting in the corner, no words arrived off his lips.

The nurse craned her head, staring into his eye. Her movement blocked Marc from seeing the man in the seat. His eye rolled to the back of his skull as his chest heaved with a pain that struck his ribs as if someone stabbed him in his side.

"Your ribs are broken. That's why it hurts to breathe."

When she moved from his line of sight, the seat was empty, and the nurse must have registered his confusion. "Still having hallucinations?"

Marc's stare darted to her. *Hallucinations? What?*

"It's a side effect from the medication. They'll wane if I don't have to sedate you again, so please try to stay calm."

Marc closed his eye and took a slow, steady breath, tracking the pain in his ribs and how much force would trigger the pain tenfold.

Obviously satisfied, the nurse said, "Good, it's about time. You've been quite the difficult one since you arrived."

She must have registered his unknowing and confused stare, because she blurted out every fine detail of his hospital stay.

"You were involved in an automobile accident. Do you remember anything about it?"

Crushing steel, heavy rain, the car flipped over, a wheel spinning. Marc nodded.

"Well, good, that's a start. The police are trying to piece together what happened, but from what we understand, you veered off the highway during a rainstorm. The car flipped over several times. You broke three ribs and hit your head pretty bad, which is why you've got that bandage wrapped around your head. We had to put in thirty staples from the back of your head, all the way to your left eye. Your head was split open like a cantaloupe. There'll be a big scar, but there are ways around it. Plastic surgery will have you looking like normal."

He went to speak, but again his words slipped down his throat with a chalky, painful wince. Marc gestured to his throat.

"Oh, the throat. We had to intubate you when you first arrived. The pain should subside over the next few days. Because of the head injury you were placed in an induced coma for three days while we assessed for potential damage to the cerebral cortex.

Fortunately, all your tests came back negative for brain damage, so we took you out of the induced coma. But that's when you became combative."

Marc mouthed the name, "Lori," and the nurse paused. Stopped cold as if she didn't want to answer or couldn't answer. Marc's heart picked up speed, thudding against his chest, confirmed by the bleep bleep bleep racing into overdrive.

She looked like she wanted to leave. Instead, she tucked the sheets beneath his legs, completely ignoring his inquiry. "The doctor will be in soon to bring you up to date on your condition."

Marc managed to squeeze a stern whisper off his lips. "Lori? Where's Lori?"

She paused again to look at the door, perhaps assessing if anyone was coming or listening. Marc followed her gaze.

"I'm not supposed to tell you," she said. "The family has requested privacy with Lori's condition, since you're not a part of the family." Another pause, and Marc was hoping she would reconsider. He waited for her to continue, watching her with intense focus. "It all just seems rather erratic and cruel. It's obvious you have a relationship with Ms. Francon."

Marc waited, his frustration escalating with the lack of information.

"I can't in good conscience, not tell you, but you didn't hear this from me. Ms. Francon suffered a hematoma. She's been in a coma since you arrived ten days ago. Her condition is listed as day to day." She paused as if she was about to add information that was not meant for Marc to hear. "She's in intensive care and has had multiple surgeries. Her mother is with her, so there's no need for you to be concerned. The best you can do is rest and heal."

Marc gritted his teeth, his jaw tight as heartbreak welled in his chest, swelling into his throat. He went to speak, but pain squeezed his throat. Instead, he mouthed the words, "I want to see her."

But the nurse said nothing. Marc waited for her reply but when none came, he mouthed the word, "Please."

The nurse shook her head. "I can't. We were given explicit instructions that only family could see her. Her mother was quite adamant about this." She looked at him and he could see there was sympathy in her eyes. "I could lose my job." She looked around the room, avoiding his stare. "It's best for you to get some rest. Now that you're coherent, you should be able to return home soon."

And with that, she walked away. Marc watched the door close with a soft thud. He looked around the room. Empty. Cold and empty, and he could feel his heart turning to stone. Turning to stone because the only other option was shattering into a million pieces. He could feel the organ hardening in his chest. Crying now, wailing, his swollen throat mattered not. He had to see her, that was all. Had to be with her no matter what Elena said. She'd been a thorn in their relationship since the beginning. That self-righteous bitch was now holding all the cards, and that fact burned his brain. Lori despised her mother. This Marc knew was true, and if Lori knew

Elena was in charge of her care and not allowing Marc to be with her, she'd more than likely kill that bitch herself.

No, he couldn't leave the hospital without seeing Lori. Not a chance in hell. But what could he do? What could he do?

As I said, killing isn't hard. Sometimes, in order to receive what is rightfully yours, killing is the path of least resistance.

15

She is going to die, Marc. That much is true. Unless you do something. But what can you do?

Marc didn't realize he was awake, his one eye open and staring. Staring into darkness. The room was pitch black and quiet. So quiet except for the soft echo of bleep bleep. So dark except for the green glow from the vitals monitor. Outside the window, the dark continued. He could hear people outside the room-nurses more than likely-shuffling back and forth and talking in whispers.

He thought he had been sleeping, considering the last thing he remembered was daylight beaming through his window, but there was no grand awakening, no jolt or gasp, as if he'd been awake the entire time. He raised his arm and noticed he was still strapped to the bedrail.

And what was with the voice? It sounded like him, but were those his thoughts? Marc did not think so, but what else could they be?

Maybe from the man in black? The one who was sitting when the nurse arrived the other day? The same man in black from his childhood.

The voice seemed to follow him wherever he went. Sleep or awake, the voice was there. And the voice spoke truth. He wanted to rip Elena's head off. Wanted to crush every bone in her face and gut her like a fuckin' pig.

The thought turned over in his head. Murder was not on his list of to-dos. But what then? Talk to her, obviously. Plead his case. Let her know they were engaged. Ready to tie the knot. Doesn't that account for something? It should, but it doesn't. The sad truth was that Elena was in control, making decisions on Lori's behalf and Marc had no seat at the table. The best he could do was take it and go home. Go home with his tail between his legs.

The hospital is releasing him tomorrow. Granted, he must pass a few tests before they sign off on his discharge, but Marc was certain he'd have no problem with any test they would throw at him. And then what? Return home to an empty apartment while knowing Lori was dying. She could be dead already for all he knew. The nurse who provided the first update had gone silent, and every other nurse and doctor was so tightlipped he wanted to rip all their heads off.

She is going to die.

He closed his eye and gritted his teeth.

What are you prepared to do, Marc?

What are you prepared to do?

Or do you plan on allowing your weak nature to drive you to the brink of insanity again? You know what happened the last time that happened? You never told Lori about it now, did you? No. And why? Because you're nothing more than a scared little boy still waiting for momma to come out of the bar.

Marc's tears dripped from his eye and all he wanted to do was scream, instead he howled like a loon, his breath stuttering across his lips.

Oh, Marc. That's what I thought.

He understood the only solution was to talk to Elena. After that, his hands were tied. It was the right thing to do, act sophisticated and maybe Elena will have a change in heart.

Unlikely, isn't it?

If he acts like a raving loon, he'll never see Lori. He sucked back his tears, inhaled the snot from his nose, and went to raise his hand to wipe the tears from his eye, but the restraint caught. He didn't even know why he was still chained to the bed.

Because of your raving and ranting and lunacy. You may have fooled Lori with your new lease on life, but not me. And not them. They know your past. It's all there in the medical record.

He tugged on the restraints, pulling as tight and as hard as he could, wanting to snap the rail in half. He started twisting in the bed, twisting and turning, trying to break free but to no avail. Marc felt like he was losing his mind, his thoughts racing like a conveyor belt set at lightning speed and he couldn't find a rational thought. No rational thought at all.

He ceased the thrashing. Stopped the tugging and pulling and rested his head on the pillow, crying like a child.

This again, Marc. Come, let me help you. What are you willing to give to have those restraints removed?

"Nothing," he screamed, whipping his head around, wanting to see. To see the man in black he knew was there. "I want nothing from you!"

Oh Marc, maybe not right now, but you will. Of course, you will, and you know it too.

Marc's breathing settled, his heart continued to race. He pursed his lips and swallowed the lump in his throat.

I remember what happened the last time you requested my help.

16

Marc remembered too. Remembered the day it started. Sitting in the car, cold and tired. People walking on the street would see him and never so much as give a second glance.

"That's Alicia's kid," they would say.

The neon lights from the bar stretched into the car like a sick and twisted night light. Marc waited in the back seat. Sometimes he'd draw, sometimes he'd color, and most often he would write. Write stories to pass the time.

Conjure the monster in his head onto the page.

The man in black had always been there. His face hidden in the shadows, but Marc could see his eyes, those blood-red eyes stained in the shadow. But to Marc, they were not the eyes of some demon come to claim his soul. They belonged to the one person he could always depend on. When he needed it the most, in those times of loneliness, when the night stretched into early morning and all he wanted to do was go home and rest beneath his covers, waiting for the dawn of a new day, the man in black was with him.

When you want someone to change and they refuse, you can always force them to see things your way. Let them know there is no other option. We use force to make them do what we want. They don't know what's good for them anyway. Always overindulging, those pitiful vermin.

Marc would sometimes sit for hours in the car, staring at the neon light glowing in the darkness. He'd listen to the chatter in the bar, the chaos rising the longer the night continued. Sometimes he'd see his mother stumble through the front door, and he'd get excited, his heart racing in his chest, ready to go home. So excited he just about bounced off the seat, but she would never so much as glance in his direction.

It's such a pity, isn't it? How some people can be so weak in their constitution they must give their souls to a substance.

And the man in black would laugh. Laugh and cackle as Marc watched his mother, her eyes lost and staring into oblivion, until some guy escorted her back into the bar.

No one cares, Marc. No one cares at all. Get used to it. When the chips are down, you'll discover they all run and hide like cockroaches from the light.

It got to the point where Marc's only friend was the man in black. Always in the shadows. Always there.

"Can you make her stop?"

Marc could hear his own voice, his younger self, as if his voice echoed across time to his adult ears.

Yes, said the man in black. *But it will take force. Are you okay with that?*

He was eight years old at the time, and he may have known little, but he knew what the word force meant.

Little Marc sucked back his tears with a sniffle. "Maybe she'll stop on her own."

A child's optimism, as naïve as it is hopeful.

He went back to his story, escaping into fiction. If he couldn't have a perfect life, he could at least write one. He heard his mother laugh when she was brought back into the bar. He tried to ignore what he heard, but he had to see. Had to see the door close. Had to confirm his hope was lost. Destroyed, just like that closed door shattered his heart.

One day, you'll be ready to make a decision on this matter. And on that day, I will be there. Just think of me, and I'll be there.

"Can you go away now?" Marc felt his tears roll down his cheeks. "I want to be alone."

To which the man in black said, "As you wish, Marc. As you wish."

Things would steadily grow worse from then on. Especially after his mother picked up the glass pipe. When you're going downhill, eventually you pick up speed and race towards the ultimate inevitability.

17

He was released in the morning. The doctor, a short, overweight man with bushy grey eyebrows, came in for a final checkup, removing the bandage and the staples from his head.

"That's a nasty scar," said the doctor. "But it'll heal in time."

The doctor, Michael Hudgense, was staring at the scar, running his tongue across his teeth. Marc could feel the weight from the scar on his skull. His left eye seemed off, as if the scar was pushing down on his eyeball. Thirty staples, and every single one hurt like a bitch when Dr. Hudgense removed them. Pressing down on the scar was like pushing needles into his brain.

And it itched like hell.

"I'll apply some antibiotic cream and a new bandage, then we'll get you discharged and on your way." He wheeled his seat over to the sink and cabinets where he started rummaging through the drawers.

Marc wanted to ask about Lori, but he knew Dr. Hudgense wasn't providing information. He'd already tried a few days ago, and Marc's response led to another reason to keep his restraints on. They removed them this morning. He assumed it didn't matter any longer. Once he's officially discharged, anything he did thereafter wasn't on their watch and Elena would have no cause to blame them for his actions. Not that it mattered to Elena. She'll more than likely have her high-powered attorney tear this place a new asshole. Not that Marc could give a shit. He'd been treated like a schizophrenic stepchild since he arrived.

Marc rubbed his scar, pressing on it while gritting his teeth. The itch was maddening.

"Oh, don't do that." Dr. Hudgense wheeled his seat over to the bed. "You could tear it open. It's a fresh wound and will take time to heal." He placed the cream on a metal tray that stood next to the bed, along with surgical tape and a roll of gauze, as Marc ceased his itching exploration. "I recommend seeing a plastic surgeon once the wound heals. When your hair grows back, it may not be so recognizable either." The doctor pinched the cream and unscrewed the cap.

"Don't bother," said Marc.

The doctor paused. "Are you sure? It may not heal properly."

Marc rubbed his scar. "I'm sure. I couldn't give a shit what I look like."

The doctor gave a smug smile and a head nod. "As you wish. I'll leave it here for you. Take it with you." He paused, staring at Marc. Staring at the scar. "In case you change your mind."

"I won't."

The doctor shrugged. "I'll leave you to it, then. Discharge papers are signed." And he paused, looking over Marc as if he were assessing Marc's next move, completely untrusting the look in Marc's eyes. "You are free to leave when you're ready. The nurses found some clothes for you. They're in the bathroom. And I do need to warn you, Mr. Saduj. Considering your history and yes, I read through your file, there is a possibility that the past may rear its ugly head." Marc shot him a confused stare, and the doctor shrugged. "Sometimes with a head injury, when the recipient is under extreme emotional stress, the past has a way of breaking open and spilling into conscious thought. Figured I'd mention that to you... considering the history." He breathed as if he needed to take a pause. "I suggest you seek weekly therapy sessions for the next six months." He stood up, eyeballing Marc.

Marc thought he was waiting for him to say something. Maybe a thank you or something along those lines, but Marc had no thank you for the doctor. All he wanted to do was punch the man in his fat fucking face. A moment later, the doctor walked out, and Marc jumped off the bed then raced to the bathroom and took the clothes out of the cabinet. He dressed quickly in a pair of dark blue sweatpants and a gray flannel shirt. His sneakers were in the bottom of the cabinet with a fresh pair of hospital socks that he stretched over his feet, then squeezed those feet into his sneakers. A plastic bag on the top shelf had his wallet. He ripped open the bag and rifled through the wallet. Everything was there. Bank card and eighty-seven dollars in cash and the picture of him and Lori. His favorite picture. Taken when the two of them were at the Halloween parade.

Marc remembered the day intimately. It was the day they both confessed their love for each other. They were dressed as

Dorothy and the Scarecrow from one of Lori's all-time favorite movies. Marc had wanted to go as vampires, but Lori won the argument. He smoothed his fingers over the picture then kissed it before squeezing it back into his wallet.

"I'm coming baby," he whispered, dropping the wallet in his pants pocket when he glimpsed a distorted human staring at him in the mirror. He thought he was looking at *Frankenstein's* monster.

It took him a second to realize he was staring at himself.

18

Jerry Hardwood tugged at his collar to release some heat from beneath his shirt. The afternoon sun was beaming through the trees as he waited for his client to arrive, listening to the songs of crickets basking in the light.

He received a phone call a few days ago with an inquiry about the house he was standing in front of. The house that was abandoned more than a century ago had been on the books in his family's company since long before he was born. But the agency never listed the property for sale, so the fact that his new client knew of its existence was odd. It came out of left field but was exactly what the business needed. Exactly what Jerry needed too, a fat check to bolster his bank account.

According to his father-who passed on to the netherworld two months ago-the house was not to be sold. Never. The why behind it was as mysterious as the house itself and, to be honest, it gave Jerry the creeps. His father, Boyd, had been tightlipped about the house, although he had whispered something on his deathbed that raised a few eyebrows.

There's a portal to hell in the basement.

Granted, the man was delusional in those final days, hopped up on painkillers and government weed. So, Jerry dismissed his father's warning and considering the family business was in dire straits, Jerry was more than willing to sell the house for a substantial amount of money to the highest bidder. He scanned across the property. The western woods stood proud and in waiting. So much land circled the house. There were over ten acres of woods. The surrounding land was also owned by the family business and came with the stipulation not to sell, which burned Jerry's britches more than he liked to admit. It was a waste of prime real estate, and, after all, they are in the real estate business, so why not release their most valued property to the developers who would come crawling out of the woodwork with offers and dreams of prosperity?

"Tons of room to build townhouses, or even houses, in this area." Jerry chewed his bottom lip, then checked his watch. Two thirty. His client was late, over thirty minutes late. He wasn't surprised though. Considering the road stopped half a mile from the house, anyone who wanted entrance would have to walk the half mile to get to the front door. Perhaps his new client hadn't expected the walk, something Jerry cursed himself for not knowing. He'd never been here, so how could he know? If he'd purchased one of those new cell phones, he would have been able to contact his client, but of course he didn't. Jerry heard about those damn phones and how the phone company was charging up the ass for service. Parting with wasted money was not in Jerry's best interest, so he decided to wait until the new fad turned into the norm, which is when those prices would come down. *Let those other fools be the guinea pigs for phone companies. I'll wait until they come back to earth to get mine.*

He wished he'd brought his water with him, though. Jerry was parched, his mouth and throat arid like desert heat. He walked around the property hoping to find a well pump or spring or anything he could find for a drop of water. But there was nothing, of course, although he was amazed at how the forest circled the property, leaving a vast open area around the house, as if the trees refused to move any closer. The ground was desolate and brown. No grass, no trees. No life. Even the birds refused to fly over the property.

He remembered his surprise when the client inquired about the house specifically. Jerry had been certain any would be developer would bulldoze that fucker to make way for affordable housing or mansions, depending on how deep the developer wanted to line his pockets. However, his new client seemed very interested in the house but not the surrounding property. He hadn't asked one question about the property. Jerry looked up at the house.

Three floors of stone and masonry looked back at him. Most of the windows had been blown out long ago, and he wondered how many kids lost their virginity over the last century within the confines of the house. He read the property description before he arrived. Upon entering the front door, there is a living room like a ballroom with a fireplace. To the left of the front door is a kitchen and a large dining room. On the right is a hallway that splits in two directions. Six bedrooms branch off the left side of the hall, and a large open room opens up on the right. There is a staircase when first entering the hallway from the ballroom. The second floor has twelve bedrooms, and the third floor is a loft or master bedroom with a cylinder-shaped room that made the house appear like a castle with its peaked roof carved from stone.

Quite the large house, but what could you actually do with it? Since electricity had not been invented when the house was built, any electrician would lose their mind trying to wire the house. Plus, Jerry was more than certain the wood had rotted a long time ago and would need to be replaced. Nope, it was better to bulldoze this fucker and start fresh.

He heard a branch snap, and he just about jumped out of his skin. His breath hitched in his throat, his heart racing into overdrive. A bead of sweat dragged across his temple to his jawline. The sound came from the front of the house. Jerry swallowed his breath with a gasp.

"That must be my guy." He shook the cobwebs from his head before trekking to the front of the house to greet his new client.

The new client who was facing the front door, all hunched over and dressed in all black. He looked like a vampire from Jerry's vantage point. His bald head gleamed in the sunlight.

Jerry cringed when the man turned to greet him. Vampire was a spot on depiction. He looked dead. His skin was pale and waxy as if he'd taken a bath in milk. His long nose gave way to beady black eyes, and his short stature made him seem more like an underprivileged child than a man. His buck teeth completed the picture, cementing Jerry's vampire theory.

Maintain, Jerry told himself. *Maintain.*

Sometimes the way a client presented turned Jerry's gut. Although, if the man has money, who gives a shit what he looks like?

Jerry offered his hand. "Mr. Field, it's a pleasure to meet you."

19

The doctor was right about one thing: it was a nasty scar. The left side of his head had been shaved and was now a carpeted fuzz attempting to take over the scar with no luck. The scar was red and swollen and stretched from the back of his head to his eye. He looked like *Frankenstein's* monster reborn. His left eye was stained red below the iris. He was disfigured, for lack of a better word.

It kept itching, and all Marc wanted to do was rip that scar off his head and itch and itch and itch. Scratch. Scratch. Scratch. Push and rub. The wound was raw and delicate. Puffy, and it hurt if he pushed too hard, but he didn't care what he looked like; all he wanted to do was see Lori. He didn't even mind the stares he received when he walked through the hall to the ICU. No one said anything to him. They simply just looked and cringed when he walked by.

He wondered if there was a picture of him in the ICU with the words: Do Not Admit written in thick black letters across his picture. He wouldn't be surprised if Elena had made the picture herself. He arrived at the closed ICU doors and paused, taking a deep breath.

"I'm here to see Lori Francon," he said, practicing for when he's asked. "I'm her cousin." His voice caught in his throat and arrived with a crack. *Yeah, her cousin with a fresh scar on his head.*

They'll never believe it. He was hoping he could slip in unnoticed and have enough time to give her a kiss and squeeze her hand to let her know he was with her.

But what if Elena is there?

Marc shook his head, then gnashed his teeth.

"Fuck it," he said and pushed the button on the wall to open the door. He breathed deeply before stepping in. "And here we go," he whispered.

First, he saw a nurse working tirelessly and distracted behind the nurses' station on his left, reading over a patient's chart. She never looked at him and he kept walking. Patient rooms were lined up across the wall on his right with glass walls. Lori wasn't in the first room, which was occupied by an older gentleman intubated and on life support. A young woman-Marc thought it was the patient's daughter-sat in a chair opposite the bed, a young man standing over her, his hand on her shoulder that the woman held as tears streamed from her eyes. She looked at Marc and cringed. Marc continued to walk.

Lori wasn't in the second room either, which featured who Marc assumed was a mother, crying over someone he thought was her daughter, completely unconscious on the bed, a nurse redressing a wound over the young girl's heart. Marc gave a quick nod, his lips pressed together, his gesture one of sympathy, but she would never know it. The mother looked at him as if he *was* Frankenstein's monster.

The third room was empty. Sunlight beamed through the windows to the neatly made bed. The room gleamed in the sunlight as if whomever recently died in this room left a bit of light, as if to show appreciation for the hard work that had been done for them. It seemed out of place among all the death and suffering.

He heard soft whispers behind him, and Marc stole a quick glance over his shoulder. A second nurse was behind the nurse's station, looking over the shoulder of the nurse Marc had seen when he first entered. They never looked at him.

Act normal, he told himself. *Keep walking.*

His stomach twisted in his gut, and his scar itched like a madman. His hand shook when he pressed against his scar, the pain butting against his skull. He stepped closer to the fourth room and stopped cold.

Lori was in the fourth room. Her eyes closed with a tube down her throat. Her face all mangled, scarred, and puffy. Attached to machines that stood over her like some mechanical god providing life where there was none. Her head was shaved and wrapped in gauze with blood stained across the left side. Marc stepped closer, his lips trembling, and noticed there was no one else in the room.

Perhaps Elena took a much needed break.

He stepped in and tapped his scar, wincing when pain shot through his brain. He went to the bed, but he couldn't believe he was looking at Lori. Her face was so swollen he second guessed himself, but he knew it was her. He took her hand, and his throat closed as he sucked back his tears.

"Lori," he whispered and leaned in with a kiss, then touched his forehead to hers. "I'm here now, baby. I'm here."

The itch started burning, and he pressed down hard on the scar. Rub. Rub. Rub. His face winced in pain, then he wiped the tears from his eyes as he squeezed Lori's hand tighter.

"Can I help you?"

The voice came from behind him, and Marc's heart sank. He said nothing, his voice caught in his throat. Rubbed that scar again and sniffled back some tears.

"You can't be in here without authorization."

He forced his words over his lips, his voice steady and controlled, fighting off the tears. Fighting off his rage. "She's my wife," he said. "I just want someone to tell me what's going on with her." He glanced at the nurse. Dark blue scrubs, short dark hair. Small stature but with hard features. She looked awestruck, as if she knew Marc had lied, but had no idea how to call him out on it. Or if she should. He was waiting for her to call security when she stepped to the other side of the bed. At least she didn't cringe like everyone else. She looked into the hallway, then looked at Marc hard and unwavering.

"I don't have time for drama," she said. "You know you can't be here, and you know she's not your wife. For whatever reason, Elena doesn't want you to see her, and we must respect her decision as the next of kin." She paused, perhaps to assess Marc's reaction, but he just stood, staring at Lori. "I will give you an update if you promise to leave." Marc turned to her. "Can you do that? Because Elena will be back soon and what none of us need-especially Lori-is an all-out battle of words and for you to be escorted off property in handcuffs. That's not going to help Lori." She paused to investigate the hall, then returned her gaze to Marc. "Agreed?"

Marc nodded as he rubbed his hand over his nose. He tapped that scar again, too.

"Ok," she said and paused again, as if regretting the deal she just made. She looked into the hall again, then turned to Marc. "Unfortunately, we can't stop the bleeding. Lori has undergone several surgeries with varying degrees of success, but the bleeding in her brain keeps returning. It's an ongoing process and her condition is listed as day to day. She's been in a coma since she arrived and unless we can stop the bleeding, the family will need to decide whether to keep her on life support." Marc scratched at the itch from his scar. "I know this is hard to hear, but there's nothing you can do for her. Go home, Mr. Saduj, and don't cause a scene."

"I want to be with her. I'll lose my mind if I go home without her. I'll be locked out of her life. How will I even know what happens to her? I can't..." His voice trailed off as he sniffled back his tears again and squeezed Lori's hand. "She would want me here with her." He looked at the nurse. "Every step of the way."

The nurse moved her head from left to right. "For the sake of my other patients and for Lori, I need you to leave Mr. Saduj."

She looked through the door again, her jaw tight. She seemed very nervous. "If you agree to go, I'll give you my direct line. You can call me, and I'll provide you with updates, but you must leave." She waited, but Marc did nothing. "Now, Mr. Saduj."

Reluctantly, Marc nodded his agreement, and the nurse released an anxious breath. Marc squeezed Lori's hand again and kissed her delicate lips. Whispered his *I love you*, then followed the nurse. She led him to the nurse's desk. She seemed fidgety and anxious, and kept looking at the entrance-perhaps to see if Elena was on her way back-as she searched around the desk. Marc was watching her, but his thoughts were with Lori.

He couldn't believe the predicament she was in. His brain twisting venomous thoughts to the forefront of consciousness with a stark and grave inevitability.

She is going to die and there is nothing you can do about it.

He gritted his teeth while listening to that voice. His voice, although he knew where it came from. The man in black was always with him, waiting in the shadow of his tragedy. A cold, clammy hand brushed across the nape of his neck, and he cringed then whipped his head around, attempting to see who was behind him. There was no one, of course. Nothing but the cold quiet of the ICU. His breathing was shallow, guttural, and he grunted out of his throat like a grovel from the grave.

"Mr. Saduj?"

He turned his attention to the nurse, who held a business card, staring at him as if he'd gone mad.

"My direct line is on the back," she said. "I'll be here for the rest of the week. Just call me once a day and I'll provide you with an update."

"Is she going to die?" Marc's voice came out like a cracked whisper. He felt like a lost child.

The nurse's hand shook, holding the card between her fingers. She paused before answering. "She's listed as day to day, but it's best to remain optimistic. Lori is a fighter. She's fighting for her life. Perhaps fighting for you, Mr. Saduj. To stay alive and live and breathe. These are critical days for her, and she needs as little drama and chaos as possible. She may be unconscious, but she can still feel and hear what is happening on the outside. Energy has a way of seeping into the fabric of our cells. It is best that all is calm around her to give her time to heal." She lifted the card again. "Here. It's best for you to rest too, Mr. Saduj."

Marc eyeballed the card trembling in the nurse's hand. He had no desire to leave. Where was he going, anyway? He had no car and no way of returning home. He'll have to haul himself to a train station to find his way back. Lucky enough, he wasn't that far away. A few hours and he'd be back in the Hollow. He took the card, albeit reluctantly, but knowing Elena was about to walk through the door turned his blood hot in his veins. The nurse was right, a verbal altercation with Elena wouldn't help Lori or her condition. It was best to take the card and leave.

"Thank you, Mr. Saduj." She stood there, staring at him, waiting for him to leave.

Marc studied the card. The nurse's name was Jessica. Her name was written in cursive with the phone number below it. He held the card like it was his last lifeline. He looked towards Lori's room, and that sinking feeling stung his heart, wondering if this was the last time he would ever see her.

She is going to die and there is nothing you can do about it.

He felt numb to his core. Helpless and alone.

And one thing was certain: Marc did not like being alone. Bad things happen when Marc is alone.

20

Mr. Field had no interest in the surrounding ten acres of property. As far as Jerry could tell, he never even looked at the property. His interest lay solely with the house, as if he'd come across a hidden gem no one in the world knew existed.

To Jerry, his new client seemed to have come home.

And what was with this new client, anyway? He may be short, but he had a voice that belonged to a giant and he held himself with a rare sophistication Jerry had only seen in his European clients. If he had to place the slight accent that traveled across Wren's lips, he would have guessed German or perhaps even a hint of Russian, although he could never be certain. Sometimes accents get lost in translation.

Wren had asked Jerry to open the door as if he wasn't aware that all he had to do was turn the knob-there was no lock on the door-the same as every teenager over the decades who had come to the house.

"Well, it is your home, Mr. Hardwood, and out of respect for your home, I must politely request for you to invite me in."

To which Jerry cocked his brows and studied the daylight. If Wren was a vampire, he'd be looking more like burnt, melted butter than a man of flesh and bone, considering the sun was strong today and out in full bloom. Jerry sensed an immediate tightness in his chest, some state of paranoia that manifested within. He swallowed his breath with a gulp down his gullet.

"Of course," he said. "Let me get the door for you." Wren stepped to the side as Jerry pushed on the double door that went no more than an inch into the house, buckled and pushed back. Quite the embarrassing moment for Jerry. He pushed again but to no avail, as if someone was behind it, keeping the door from opening. He regarded Wren briefly. "It must be stuck." But his voice trailed off when he saw the dark clouds rolling towards them as the wind kicked up a few notches. Wren was standing like a statue, his right hand held palm up across his stomach. Jerry noticed his long fingers and pointy fingernails, and the look in his eyes, those beady eyes, stretched wide with anticipation.

Jerry had a fleeting thought to run and hide and forget about the money. This was all too weird. Thought about telling Wren he'll have to come back another day-yeah, when Jerry can have a few people with him-because the door won't budge.

You're being paranoid. Just get the damn door open.

He cursed himself for not opening the door while he waited for Wren. He must be getting rusty. Normally, Jerry would have gone through every inch of the house prior to his client's arrival, but he truly believed this meeting was about the surrounding property and not the abandoned house. The house that creaked under the wind's gale when Jerry noticed the sun had disappeared, washed away by dark threatening clouds. Now the rain started. Sporadic raindrops slapped against the porch and now he really thought differently about entering the house. Being stuck in a dilapidated and abandoned mansion in the middle of the woods during a rainstorm with a stranger who looked like a vampire was not how he planned to spend his afternoon.

The things you do for money.

Jerry pushed his shoulder into the door, hoping with every fiber of his being that the door would not budge.

So why am I still pushing?

The door swung open, and Jerry fell to the ground as the doors slapped against the back walls. Jerry swallowed a mouthful of dust and dirt, which did nothing for his arid throat. He coughed something awful, on his knees on the dust and dirt covered wooden floor. The sky grew dark as he rose to his feet, coughing and brushing the dirt off his pants and shirt.

He was in the ballroom. The room was vast with a fireplace that looked like it had seen better days on the wall leading to the hallway. The ceiling was low, and Jerry was well aware the stairs would be cramped. Claustrophobic is how Jerry described it. He knew about these old mansions. They always squeezed any host or guest with their cramped walls and tight spaces. He noticed Wren never said a word. Jerry regarded his new client, who stood at the entrance looking in as if he could not cross the threshold. He turned to Jerry with an anxious stare, as if his anticipation had reached a fever pitch and he couldn't wait any longer to enter the home.

"C'mon in. You are more than welcome." He gestured for Wren to enter and the sudden smile that crossed Wren's lips turned Jerry's gut.

Wren closed his eyes when he said, "Thank you, Mr. Hardwood," and stepped across the entrance when thunder raged above the house with a howling wind that tore through the open doors. The same wind that pressed against the nape of Jerry's neck like a hand that cringed Jerry's bones, cascading down his spine.

Jerry didn't know where to begin. There wasn't much to say, considering the house was in shambles, with dust and dirt covering just about every inch of the floors and windowsills, and cobwebs draped across the walls and ceiling. Sure, a huge renovation job would bring the house back to life, but what was there to see now? So, he said the only thing he could think of. "Is there a part of the house you'd like to see more than the others? Like the master bedroom? We can start up there and make our way down if you like."

Now the heavens opened, dousing the house with sheets of rain as the wind rifled through the open windows. Wren was looking over the house, standing tall and erect with his hand in front of him, still palm up.

"Wren?" Jerry said, attempting to snap Wren's focus and get this tour started when Wren trained his beady eyes on Jerry. "Should we start in the master bedroom? Is there any room you'd like to see first?"

To which Wren grinned and said, "Yes, Mr. Hardwood. I'd like to see the basement first."

21

Marc heard the train horn before he could feel the wind across his skin. He noticed his scar itched when the wind raced across it, and he clenched his teeth. That itch was maddening.

He was thinking about Lori while he waited for the train. He couldn't get the image out of his head. Lori unconscious with a tube down her throat. He couldn't believe he actually left.

Because you're weak, Mr. Saduj.

The voice was like a whisper that erupted in the center of his brain. He couldn't get rid of it, and he knew the man in black would not relent. It was best to accept his presence. At least for now.

Something cold and heavy brushed across the nape of his neck, and Marc cringed while gritting his teeth.

She is going to die and there is nothing you can do about it. You have no power. No control. You can't even stand up and take your rightful place by her side.

Marc looked up from the platform as the train screeched to a stop and noticed the child staring at him, holding his mother's hand, waiting to board the train. Quite apparent that the boy was staring at his scar. The scar that Marc could feel like a thick impression that pressed against his skull. He could feel it now, pulsing and throbbing. He could feel it like pressure on his brain, and it itched like a son of a bitch. Marc pushed on his scar and his vision blurred. Felt like his eyeball was going to pop out of his skull. Something wet dripped across his eye, and he saw the boy cringe.

Looked at his fingers and saw blood on the tips.

"Fuck," his voice a whine. Felt like he was about to cry. His head now pounded in his skull. Felt like his brain was bruised. He pressed his forearm against the scar, the pain like needles in his skull. His vision blurred once again, so he closed his eyes when the train doors dinged and opened, and he kept dragging his arm across the scar. After he'd satisfied his itch, he looked at his forearm and saw blood on his shirt. Just a bit, but not enough to go back to the hospital.

Marc sniffled back his tears, watching the boy and his mother board the train. The boy continued to stare from over his shoulder. The mother paid them no mind. Marc could feel his tears threatening to unleash, his bottom lip quivering.

Pitiful! So, so pitiful.

Marc stepped onto the train and took an empty seat away from the other passengers. He stared at the doors, tension building in his veins, watching, waiting for the doors to close. He hated that those doors were about to close. Confirmation that he has truly left his beloved. Was he abandoning Lori? Marc's heart wrenched in his chest.

Pitiful isn't the word. Look at you. So weak. As weak as that child who sneered at you. So, so helpless. Can't you do anything? Anything at all? Can't you take control? Tsk. Tsk. Tsk. You are the meek and unworthy.

Marc heard the familiar ding on the door, and he snapped his head around, eyeballing the door that slid closed with a scrape and a thud. Marc tightened his jaw, gritting his teeth. The train jolted forward. Jolted forward and kept moving, gliding smoothly out of the station.

Marc couldn't help the tears that welled in his eyes. He wiped those tears and held his hand over his mouth, stifling his cries. He noticed the boy was still staring at him. Marc turned to the window, watching the rolling hills and trees turn into blurs as he rested his head against the window, cold and defeated.

Pitiful. I haven't seen you this pitiful since the night you asked for my help. So defeated and meek. The night you asked me to take care of your mother.

22

Jerry wavered back and forth as if the wind attempted to push him over. His gaze steadily locked in on Wren's beady eyes.

The basement. Basement. In the basement. Basement. There's a portal to hell in the basement.

"You want to see the basement?"

"Yes, Mr. Hardwood. That is what I said."

"The basement."

There's a portal to hell in the basement.

Wren grinned. A knowing, conniving grin as if he had captured Jerry's gaze and refused to relent, grinning because he knew he had him. The heavens rolled with a thunderous boom. The wind howled through the open door with a wallop of air that wrapped around Jerry, tightening his spine. Darkness crawled across the floor and ceiling, creaking the foundation and strangling the light. The same darkness that crept across Wren, casting him in a blanket of shadow. Elusive and menacing, Wren's eyes, those steady, beady eyes, pierced into Jerry's mind like a talon that captured his thoughts, words, and reflexes.

The basement. There's a portal to hell in the basement.

Wren cocked his head to the right, his gaze never leaving Jerry. "Perhaps you require assistance?" He paused as Jerry wavered in the wind. Seemed Jerry lost his powers of speech, and his thoughts emptied from his mind as if Wren had pulled a plug and all his thoughts funneled down the drain. "Allow me to show you the way."

Rain showered through the open door and windows, pelting the ground with a fierce, unrelenting spatter. Thunder rolled across the house, shaking the walls. Lightning cast a sliver of blue light across Wren's features.

Those eyes. Those eyes carried millenniums filled with torture and knowing. Jerry tried to break free from Wren's supernatural shackle. Tried to turn his eyes away when a wet pressure pressed against the nape of his neck. His eyes drifted, his head light, eyelids heavy.

Wren's grin, his beady eyes, unwavering, steady and cold.

A kiss from Wren's lips, blown across the wind to Jerry's eyes. He felt himself fall. Falling back. Pain raced across his neck and spine when he dropped like a sack of bricks. Saw the wooden floor, wet and slick from the rain.

Thunder.

Lightning.

Howling wind.

Shutters rapped against the walls.

Wren's stare, captivating. Mesmerizing.

There's a portal to hell in the basement.

"No worries, Mr. Hardwood." Wren cocked his head. "I'll bring you there." The wind howled through the house like a wolf ready to devour its prey. Wren looked up, closing his eyes.

"It really is such a delight to see."

23

Detective Stephen Carver had seen more than his share of depravity, adversity, and violence in his more than thirty years as a detective in the Sleepy Hollow Police Department.

In his time, he'd seen it all. Murder, suicides, murder suicides, runaways who wound up bound and gagged and sold to the cartels for sex trafficking. He'd found a few in Mexico just this past winter. Assault and battery, domestic violence, kids taking the bullying way too far and every once in a while, the victim took matters into their own hands and showed those bullies just what true fear was all about. Yeah, he'd seen a thing or two in his time. So, when Detective Stephen Carver arrived at the scene of Sleepy Hollow's latest crime, he gave the situation no real credence other than the fact that it was just another crime. Another report to be filed and another family whose heart was about to crack open like a fissure through the moon.

Police cruisers were parked up and down North Washington Street in Sleepy Hollow. The uniforms were keeping the public at bay. Carver cased the scene; a toothpick wedged in the corner of his mouth. He scanned across the road and alley. He always assessed the scene first. Sometimes the murderer would be in attendance, watching the police puzzle over their work. Caver was looking for anyone in the crowd that appeared suspicious. There were none.

He'd been informed that the body was found late this morning when the fry cook for the Sleepy Hollow Tavern went to toss the garbage. According to the report, he tossed the garbage, then lit up a cigarette when he saw the body. Or the remains of a body, at least. The cook-a young tike named Chris Polov-said he'd puked all over the alley. He couldn't take the smell nor the gruesome method that had claimed the poor girl's life. Obviously, he wasn't expecting a dead body when he woke up this morning.

Carver could see the blood on the back wall of the tavern. He looked up then, his eyes roaming to the heavens and the rolling dark clouds threatening to wash away his evidence. It looked like the storm stalled over the western woods, although he knew it wouldn't hold. He could smell the storm in the air. He stepped to the scene, flagging down a uniformed officer.

"Yes, sir." The boy looked like he graduated from high school last year. M. Chavez was written on his uniform.

"Tarps," Carver said.

"Come again?"

Carver looked up. "It's gonna piss rain all over us in about a half hour, give or take. I need you to touch base with dispatch and get them to bring tarps large enough to cover the alley. We need to keep the place as dry as possible if we're going to take proper evidence."

Chavez looked up to the rolling dark sky.

"You got that, officer?" Carver asked as he stepped towards the crime scene.

"I'm on it, sir."

Carver gave him the thumbs up over his shoulder. "You're the man. Thank you."

The smell of rain clung to the asphalt as the wind rifled through the street. Carver weaved between the officers standing on the sidewalk, most of whom gave him an unsteady stare, as if they pitied the man for what he was about to see. It could be the old race card too. Some white officers still took offense that Carver's skin color did not reflect their own, although most accepted him for who he was. A man with a bloodhound nose and an uncanny knack to see between the lines to the truth. Most couldn't give a shit what color he was. Racism being the mark of a devolved mind, a kind of calling card to depravity, sin, and irrational thought fueled by anger towards the self and a false belief in superiority.

He paid those devolved cockroaches no mind and went on with his duty as he came closer to the yellow tape strewn across the alley's entrance. The alley was ten feet wide, splitting the divide between the tavern and a chain-link fence that separated the alley from a vacant lot. He ducked under the tape. A mix of uniformed officers, EMTs, and investigators surrounded the body, talking, snapping pictures, and gathering evidence. The talk was quiet, more like whispers. The storm rolled with booming thunder and Carver looked up at the sky that darkened the scene. He rolled his toothpick to the opposite side of his mouth then looked at the body lying on the ground next to the back of the tavern.

Like a bloodhound, he stepped towards the body and the officers parted like the Red Sea.

The victim-a female no more than twenty-five years old-lied on her back, looking up at the dark sky. Her eyes were wide open, and her face carried a surprised expression filled with horror. Carver's first clue. More than likely, she didn't know the murdering bastard. The expression reflected that the perp surprised the victim. Carver squatted beside the body. There was a gaping hole in the victim's chest. Her heart had been removed.

How?

Removing a heart would take some type of tool. Some medical instrument to crack the chest bone, but her expression is off. If a tool was used, she would have known it was coming. Her teeth would be grinding, but her mouth is wide open as if in shock. And this gaping hole suggests someone's fist punched through the chest. He scanned around the body.

No blood. Maybe this was done somewhere else, and the body dumped in this location. But why? Something to do with the tavern?

Carver chewed on his toothpick, studying the wall with the pentagram drawn in blood, and the peculiar words written beneath the pentagram:

Humanitatis finis ut novum principium.

"Now what the hell does that mean?"

"Humanity's end as a new beginning."

Carver looked over his shoulder at Detective Montgomery. "You sure?"

"I called it in, sir. Took some time, but dispatch was able to decipher the meaning. It's Latin." He gestured to the writing beside the body where the words **Initium Novum** were written above her head. "And that one means, *A New Beginning*."

Carver nodded and returned to the body. He studied her chest, and the fear forever plastered in her pupils. It didn't make sense. Not one iota. A procedure like that would take time, but her expression turned his gut and tingled his instincts. Carver stood up, his eyes on the pentagram and Latin phrase written in blood, before he turned to Montgomery.

"Go to the hospital. Find a heart surgeon and find out what it would take for someone to punch through a chest bone."

Montgomery looked at him as if he were crazy. "You think someone punched a hole in her chest and tore out her heart? That's a bit of a stretch, don't you think?"

Carver rolled his toothpick into the corner of his mouth. "When it comes to murder, in my experience at least, never assume something can't be done."

Montgomery nodded, his lips curled into his mouth. "Okay. I'm on it."

Carver looked at the sky and the rolling clouds inching closer to his crime scene. "And find out where my tarps are."

24

Wren escorted Jerry down the hall where ancient stones made up the walls with their dark and foreboding visage. To Jerry, those stones seemed to crawl and slither as if they carried a sinister soul foaming at the mouth to be released. The storm roared through the house, creaking the foundation as if the house could collapse with the next large gale. Darkness crept across the stone hallway, growing darker the further they walked when the wall sconces-two on the opposing walls guarding the entrance one of which was by the stairs leading to the second floor, two in the middle, and a pair at the end of the hall opposite the two closed doors on opposite sides of the hall-burst with fiery life. Jerry could hear the flames crackle and roar.

"We must remain confident, poised, and always ready," said Wren, his right arm wrapped around the small of Jerry's back, his left hand in that familiar position, draped across his stomach, palm up. Jerry's head lolled to the side towards Wren. He was sweating profusely, and every step forward seemed to turn up the heat. He could feel the wind across his back, but it no longer provided a reprieve, as if the wind burned across his skin, amping up the heat index. "The master will be here soon, and we must be prepared for his arrival. Do you understand, Jerry? Are you hearing me?"

Jerry's voice arrived monotone and flat. "Prepare for the coming of the master. All must be ready for his arrival."

"Yes, Jerry. Yes, indeed."

They arrived at the end of the hall, and Jerry craned his head, staring at the wall. Wren reached his hand to the sconce and gently pulled it down when the wall in front of them creaked and popped open, just an inch, but enough for Wren to slither his long fingers around. He pulled the door open, stepping himself and Jerry back a step to allow the door to open fully. Eternal darkness existed beyond the open door. He couldn't see more than two inches past the entrance.

"Watch your step," said Wren, pushing on the small of Jerry's back. Guiding him towards the darkness but Jerry's feet stopped cold. He could feel Wren's gaze, those beady eyes staring. "Oh, no worries for you, Jerry. You'll be taken care of. The master always repays his servants."

Jerry could hear his own shallow breath as he stepped through the door. Stepped through onto a wide and long spiraling staircase. The steps were made of stone, with no banister or railing on the right. On the left was the wall made from the same stone. Jerry looked to his right as Wren guided him down the steps. Seemed like a forty-foot drop into darkness when the sconces all roared with life, one after the other, all the way down the steps, revealing a wide-open circular room, with a tall ceiling that reached high over their heads. Jerry wasn't certain, but his first thought was that he was walking into a dungeon. He could hear chains rattling, and heavy whines that were cut off suddenly as if those throats feared being cut. Shadows crept across the walls, slithering with a whispered groan as if they were waiting in anticipation to be released. The souls of the tortured captured in a stone prison.

There's a portal to hell in the basement.

The air was musty and choked the throat with heat and dust. Jerry's legs wobbled, growing heavy and weary with each step. He noticed Wren hadn't said a word since they stepped onto the staircase and when he looked at Wren, his eyes were wide, his lips parted, baring those large buck teeth. Jerry wasn't certain if that was a grin across Wren's lips or if he was breathing heavy, the air was so thick and hot, his chest lifting with each thick breath. He could feel the sweat on his forehead and how it dripped across his skin, beading off his nose and jawline when they reached the bottom step.

"Here," said Wren, leaning Jerry against the wall. "Stay here." Jerry nodded, leaning his head against the hot stone. Wren turned to the open room that stretched on for a hundred feet. Beneath the top of the stairs were openings that led into darkness. Entrances-three of them-with pointed tops that stretched high above to the top of the steps. He could have sworn the darkness that filled those entrances moved and slithered and swirled. And the energy. The energy infested Jerry's cells as if he swallowed pure evil.

Wren stretched his arms as if he could embrace the room, his fingers stretched like talons and flexing as he stopped in the center, turning slowly to those three entrances. He gazed into their dark depths.

"Lead me, my master," Wren whispered as he closed his eyes and breathed deeply. "I bend to your will. Lead my hand, my senses, and my heart."

Jerry forced his eyes open. There was a light on beyond those three entrances, like the glow of a distant fire. Wren took three steps forward, then paused, looking down at his foot that rubbed against the stone floor. One of those stones wobbled when he pressed his foot against it and the firelight dissipated, returning darkness to those rooms. Wren was on his knees now, his fingers inching around the stone that he heaved up and over, laying the stone on the floor as he looked inside.

"Oh, my master. You make all things new." He squatted around the hole, reaching his arms in and heaved out a large crystal bowl, placing it beside him on the floor. Reached in again and pulled out a raggedy old cloth that clearly had something wrapped in it. Wren unraveled the cloth, revealing a mallet made from wood with an etching around it that Jerry thought looked like veins. Wren's excitement crawled across his face. He looked like a man possessed. "Thank you, master. Thank you." He coddled the mallet like a baby, then kissed the top before gently placing the mallet on the cloth to the side of the bowl. He looked in further, then reached his arm in, up to his shoulder. He was searching. Searching and finding when his arm ceased moving and he pulled a second cloth wrapped object from the hole.

"The unholy wine. The transformative drink." Wren unwrapped the cloth to reveal the bottle that lay within as he dropped the cloth behind him and held the bottle to the light. Green liquid sloshed inside the bottle. Written in thick black letters on the crinkled label was the word Absinthe. Wren's breath stuttered in his throat. "All is as you said it would be. All is right. Initium Novum. The human's end begins on this night with an evolution towards slavery. My master at the helm." Wren's head turned to Jerry. Those beady eyes devouring every inch of him. "And me, a god by his side." His grin stretched across his lips as a foul laugh erupted from his throat.

Jerry couldn't take the heat any longer. He slid across the wall and dropped onto the steps. His ribs cracked when he hit those stones and pain raced to his brain as he bounced off the steps, then flopped back down. Wren stood, holding the bottle as if it were his last lifeline.

"We have much to do, Jerry."

Marc Saduj.

"The property must be secured."

Marc Saduj.

"The name you hear is being whispered to you by the master." Wren looked up to the ceiling as if he could see the sky beyond. "He has been banished to the ether. Forced to walk the earth in limbo." Jerry noticed the howl from the storm, like a thousand wolves calling to the moon. "A ghost. My master has endured the pain of absence for far too long."

Marc Saduj.

"The name he whispers shall be the sole proprietor of this home. The property. Even the trees who have waited centuries for the master's return."

Marc Saduj.

"Do this for him and he will reward you with more than you have ever dreamed."

Marc Saduj.

"Soon, Jerry. Soon his union will manifest in flesh and bone and brought to fruition by the stayed hand of love… then returned with blood." Wren was in front of him, staring into his eyes. When he had moved, Jerry didn't know. "And this home… his beacon to Xibalba." Wren looked at the bottle of green cradled in his arms. "Our time has come, Jerry. Your lineage is made right tonight. Go," he said, taking Jerry's wrist and lifting him with gentle ease. "Listen to the master's call and he will lead you back to me, where your reward is waiting. I shall remain here." He turned to the room. "I must offer the sacrifice before the master's return." He touched his pocket and closed his eyes. "An offering of a soul to Xibalba." He turned to Jerry. "Do you understand, Jerry?"

"Listen to the master's whisper. He will lead me back to you."

"Indeed." Wren reached his arm to Jerry's shoulder, turning him to the steps. "Go, now, Jerry. Time is of the essence. Tonight, you redeem your ancestors and their ancient grudge."

Jerry took the steps up, understanding his mission. He had no other thought, as if all his thoughts were drained from his mind. All except one. The whisper. The whisper was all he could hear.

Marc Saduj.

When he reached the top step, he looked down to see Wren dragging a pedestal from beneath the steps into the center of the room.

25

The train hobbled along the tracks into the Tarrytown Train Station. Marc's stop. He was eager to get back to his apartment and call for an update. Sure, he'd been at the hospital a few hours ago, but in such cases, conditions could change at any moment. It was best to stay updated. Marc stood by the door, waiting for the train to stop, when he noticed how dark the sky was, but the storm seemed to hover in the west. He hoped to be home before the downpour. His apartment was a short ten-minute walk from the train station, and when that door dinged and scraped open, he made a beeline towards his home.

The storm blackened the sky with thick dark clouds that crawled towards him as if the clouds meant to sneak up on the world before unleashing its fury. Marc kept his eyes on the storm as he pounded pavement, his heart jumping in his chest. His apartment building was made from brick and concrete and stood six stories high. Thunder growled from those clouds when Marc opened the foyer door and stepped in, then keyed into the glass door that opened into the building. His fingers and hand trembling as he turned the lock and heard the dead bolt click open. He pushed through the door into the hall and was about to race to the stairs when the first apartment on his left opened with a sudden rush, stopping Marc in his tracks.

Mrs. Leiter stood in the doorway holding a plastic garbage bag and a startled stare. She was a short lady with bluish-gray hair that swirled on top of her tiny round cranium. Her large glasses sat at the edge of her long, pointed nose. Two beady blue eyes stared at him through those glasses. Her skin was like parchment paper-crinkled and thin-and covered in liver spots. Her loose and fattened cheeks dropped to her jawline, obviously losing their battle with gravity. She wore a thick black sweater, and long brown pants all bunched up beneath her overhanging stomach.

The last thing Marc needed right now was Mrs. Leiter. The woman gave him the creeps and always had. Her voice was raspy, assaulting the ears with an unrelenting barrage of complaints and suffering. And whatever she was holding in that plastic garbage bag smelled foul, like rotting meat. Must be Mr. Leiter's diapers. Marc was sure of it. For what else could cause such an insidious stench?

And she was staring, dumbfounded and startled, as if she'd been caught red-handed for some crime old ladies like to indulge in. Her cheeks turned rosy and blushed. Marc noticed his scar began to itch and throb.

"My dear Marc, what has happened to you?" Her mouth hung open as if she was in awe of his scar-it was all she would look at. "You look like *Frankenstein's* monster."

Something moaned from deep within Mrs. Leiter's apartment. Some shudder that shook the walls and Marc watched Mrs. Leiter grip that garbage bag tight as her body tensed and her nose crinkled, staring at Marc with a scowl that turned his stomach sickly.

"Those damn pipes again," she said, as if she said whatever thought first crossed her mind. Marc didn't like the look in the old woman's eyes. A stare that sent shivers down his spine. Mrs. Leiter had always been nosy and creepy. Her family owned the apartment building since it was built more than a hundred years ago and Mrs. Leiter and her husband, Ben, have lived in their apartment since way before Marc was born. She had been good friends with Marc's mother, always visiting in the afternoon for a drink or coffee. Mrs. Leiter enjoyed a stiff scotch, and judging by the pungent smell lifting off her breath, Marc was certain she still did.

"They'll be the death of me." Mrs. Leiter swayed on her feet, gripping that garbage bag closer to her hip. "Well, have at it boy, what happened to you?"

Marc let his defenses drop. It's better to placate the woman and be gone a moment later. "I was in an accident, Mrs. Leiter, but I'm fine now. The scar will heal."

"Going to need some plastic surgery on that one."

"Something like that. Look, I've got an important phone call to make. Enjoy your day, Mrs. Leiter." And with that he shuffled to the steps, gripping both banisters, his foot on the first step when he stopped cold. He could feel Mrs. Leiter's gaze on his back. Felt heat on the nape of his neck, like a dark energy that gripped his bones and squeezed, turning those hairs on his neck erect.

He inched his head around and Mrs. Leiter was standing, staring, her eyes devouring him, those beady eyes like daggers in his back as her lips curled in the corners of her mouth into a sickly tightlipped grin. And then the bag moved. Just a bit, and Mrs. Leiter gripped that bag even closer to her hip.

"Just a rat," she said and waved him off. "Just a rat." Marc remembered that every time Mrs. Leiter's anxiety kicked in, her voice inflection changed to a high-pitched whine.

It didn't look like a rat and Marc could swear the old lady was losing it. Perhaps a little at a time, but all her marbles were definitely jumping out of her brain one sane marble at a time. Marc shook his head and took the steps to his apartment, all the while feeling her presence as if she earned a permanent space in his brain and he couldn't shake the sensation that she was watching him. When he arrived on his floor, he could hear her shuffling down the hall to the basement door, dragging the garbage bag across the floor.

"Fuckin ladies weird," he whispered, shaking his head as he keyed into his apartment when he heard a whack from the first floor that reverberated up the steps. His hand stopped cold, hovering over the doorknob. Another whack, as if Mrs. Leiter was beating her garbage with a stick. He could hear her laugh, low and guttural, as if satisfied with the whacking beating of her garbage bag. Marc stood in the hall, listening with his door propped open.

What is in that garbage bag? Maybe it is a rat, and she's beating it to death?

Now he could hear her dragging the bag towards the basement door. With every pull across the tile, Mrs. Leiter huffed that low sinister groan.

Marc entered his apartment and closed the door, then slapped the dead bolt into a locked position and stepped away as if Mrs. Leiter could come barreling into his apartment. He stood in the small foyer, staring at the door.

"Why does she have to be so frigin weird?" He swallowed his breath with a thick wallop down his throat. Staring, waiting in silence when he turned to the kitchen on his right and dropped his keys on the counter then stepped into the living room.

The kitchen had two points of entry, the first in the foyer by the front door, and the second led into the living room. No dining room, but Marc had a small table tucked in the corner of the already cramped kitchen. A couch and recliner chair sat in front of a brown coffee table. His television sat on a desk by the wall closest to him. Across the living room on the opposite wall were two windows that led to the fire escape. A hallway led further into the apartment from the wall with the television, with the master bedroom at the end of the hall, the bathroom before the master and the second bedroom was the first down the hall.

Marc had turned the second bedroom into an office for writing, and he slept there most nights when Lori wasn't with him, on the small couch tucked in the corner of that room. The master bedroom was simple, a king bed and armoire-the one he purchased from Lori's antique shop-were the only furniture in the master bedroom.

He sat on the recliner and gripped the yellow rotary phone off a small round table next to the chair. Reached into his pocket and retrieved the business card, dialing the number with shaky fingers when the thunder cracked above the building and Marc looked over his shoulder through the windows. The clouds turned day into night, rolling over the Hudson River and crawling across the Tappan Zee Bridge. The two landmarks were prominently displayed through Marc's window.

The phone rang in his ear, his apartment growing darker with the coming storm, waiting for the nurse to pick up. But she didn't. The call went to an answering machine where the nurse provided her name and a promise to return the call. Marc left a message with his phone number and hung up. He sat for a long while, rocking back and forth, listening to the thunder. The creak from his recliner whistled as he rocked.

He eyeballed the bottle of scotch on the table in the kitchen and stopped rocking. The creak echoed into the room.

Have a drink, he told himself. *I need to settle my nerves.*

And Marc did just that, his scar itching and he did all he could to ignore it. He didn't want it to bleed again. It'll never heal if it keeps bleeding. His skull was on fire, his scar itching with mad fever as he fixed himself a stiff drink and returned to his recliner, turning it around to watch the storm.

Watch the storm and wait to hear from the nurse.

26

Detective Carver watched as firemen raised the tarp over his crime scene. Just in time too, the storm was about to unleash holy hell on Sleepy Hollow. Forensics officers were working at lightning speed, trying to beat the storm. He rolled that toothpick to the corner of his mouth while scanning every fine detail of the crime scene.

He knew the area well and was certain the girl had been killed somewhere else and the body dumped in this location. Considering last night was a Friday, the street had to be jumping with people. The fact that someone could get away with dumping a body in the middle of all that chaos was against the odds. Plus, he was certain the bar's staff had to come out every so often to smoke a cigarette or throw out garbage and would have noticed a dead girl in the alley. The bars close in this area by four A.M., although he knew some stayed open for at least a few hours more, officially closing just before dawn. Which didn't give a lot of time before twilight beamed across the city, illuminating any would-be murdering pig and his body dumping exploits.

He wondered what the medical examiner would determine was the time of death. Considering how fresh the body looked, he was certain it hadn't been more than a few hours. Carver looked over at the body that was now being zipped up into a plastic body bag and brought to the coroner. He'll be making a visit there later today once he's finished his investigation.

But who is she? And how is she connected to the tavern?

There was no identification found on the body, and none of the bar staff could identify the victim. They all had the same story. They'd never seen her before. Perhaps she's a runaway? Caught in the dregs with some unsavory characters.

But what's with the hole in the chest?

Carver was almost certain his hunch about punching a hole in the girl's chest was inaccurate, considering he was skeptical that a man could punch a hole through a chest bone, even if the sonofabitch was hopped up on speed. Plus, the fact that the hole was clean and perfectly round indicated a tool was used to perform the surgery. Which led to the next question:

What did they do with the heart?

"Detective Carver?"

Carver turned on his heels. Detective Montgomery was walking towards him. "Perfect timing. What'd you find?"

Montgomery stopped walking and flipped the small notebook he was holding open. "Spoke to a heart doctor and he assured me that punching a hole through someone's chest would take the strength of ten men. Not that it couldn't happen with repeated thrusts, but that would take a bit of time to accomplish. He also said there would be additional bruising and, considering the chest bone could splinter, the possibility of additional blood from the murderer's fist would be on the body." He was shaking his head. "Doesn't seem possible, detective, but he was put off by the hole in the chest. Couldn't fathom what type of tool would have been used. He's never heard of a tool to accomplish a perfectly round opening. It's a puzzle he couldn't piece together." He flipped his notebook closed.

Carver gnawed on his toothpick, thinking.

"It's a strange one detective." Montgomery looked over at the crime scene. The EMTs wheeled the body away on a gurney as thunder rolled across the sky and lightning pumped within dark clouds. The wind blew fierce with a howl through the street and raindrops fell in thick strands across the tarp.

"What're you thinking?" asked Montgomery.

Carver turned to the crime scene that was now getting doused in rain. Those tarps were doing their job, but unfortunately, the rain was now dripping down the tavern's wall, seeping through the crevices in the tarp and across the pentagram. Carver watched as the blood streamed towards the ground. He was grateful he had forensics dust for prints on the pentagram when he first arrived. Grateful they completed their examination, and those results were headed off to the medical examiner's office.

Another howling wind whipped across the alley as the rain arrived in droves. Detective Carver didn't know what to think, not yet at least. This was an enigma, and he will need to puzzle it out. But for now, he said the only thing that made the most sense, "I'm thinking we should get out of the rain," and he did just that, moving beneath the tarp to continue whatever investigation he could. He rolled that toothpick to the corner of his mouth, his skin moist as the wind howled beneath the tarp, watching the rain erase his evidence.

It made the building look like it was bleeding.

27

The whispers drove his actions. Jerry made the half-mile trek back to his car as if he were a robot with one single command: get back to the office and complete the necessary paperwork. He drove with mindless abandon, numb and mesmerized, those whispers in his ear, always so close. He could feel hot breath on his neck, and he received more than a few concerned stares from his staff when he entered his office.

"You look so pale, Jerry. Maybe you should go home for the day."

"Are you okay, sir? You don't look so good."

Jerry knew what they were referring to. During the drive over, he caught his reflection in the rearview mirror, his skin flushed and ghostly pale and moist with perspiration. His clothes were wet, saturated with rain and glued to his body. The skin around his eyes was sunken and red, as if his eyes were burning inside his skull. His pupils constricted and squeezed into the size of a pin. He had no reaction and kept driving.

Give it all to Marc Saduj. Marc Saduj. The property, sign it all over to Marc Saduj.

"Yes, as you wish."

"Who are you talking to?" This was Lindsey. She's worked for the agency for the better part of two decades. "Are you sure you're, okay? You look like you've seen a ghost."

Jerry gritted his teeth, staring mindlessly at Lindsey.

You're fine. Doing great. Simply wonderful.

"Simply wonderful," Jerry said, his voice monotone and robotic.

Lindsey's eyes narrowed as she cocked her head back.

Bring the file. Get the paperwork completed.

Jerry eyeballed Lindsey. "Get the paperwork completed. Bring the file to me."

"Okay, then." Lindsey paused a moment, assessing Jerry. All he did was stare straight ahead, as if she wasn't in the same room. Staring off into oblivion. She quietly left the office and closed the door behind her. Jerry watched her through the office windows. The front wall of his office was all windows, providing a clear view of the reception area where Lindsey was instructing Claire-the help Jerry hired a month ago.

She suspects the worst. Something foul and sinister beneath the fold.

Jerry felt pressure across the nape of his neck as if a cold hand wrapped around his bones. He turned to his window when the rainstorm howled. The sky was dark and growing darker, the wind in high gear, whipping the bushes outside his window into a heated frenzy, as the thunder cracked and groaned across the sky. Lightning splintered and pumped within black clouds as rain pelted his window. But all he could hear was the trickling of that rain into the storm drain in the parking lot.

Trickling down.

That pressure on his neck turning his limbs immobile as if telling him not to move. To stay put and not move even one little muscle. He scanned across the room, his eyes flitting from one side to the other. This was his father's office. He grew up here, and it always felt like a second home. The handprint turkey he'd made in kindergarten was still hanging from the wall, faded and frayed at the edges. Family pictures and his father's awards for his dedicated service to Sleepy Hollow and Tarrytown surrounded the turkey print. Jerry clenched his fists over the desk when the pressure squeezed around his neck. He licked his dry lips.

There's a portal to hell in the basement.

The basement. You want to see the basement?

Wren's beady eyes staring at him. Even now, in this room, he could see them. Watching. Staring. Assessing his thoughts and intentions while he squeezed his fists so tight his knuckles were turning white. Howling wind raced across the windows as those bushes scrapped against them. A stuttered breath in his throat, he tried to force it down.

He could feel Wren's arm across the small of his back, leading him down the stairs. He could see the bottle of Absinthe, green and glowing inside the bottle. How he longed for a drink of it now. To settle his nerves. His throat was so parched, he could drink from a fountain of Absinthe while watching Lindsey and

Claire working diligently behind the receptionist's desk. Speaking in whispers to each other, their eyes wandering every so often, stealing a glance into his office. A glance at him. His fists jerked with a sudden twitch.

Perhaps your staff requires a lesson.

Perhaps they suspect you're not in your right mind.

Raindrops pelted his windows as the wind swirled with a fierce fever across the parking lot. He watched his staff with the intensity of a predator as a thick pang of anger wriggled into his brain. Lindsey had always been a know it all, questioning every decision his father had ever made. Questioned him too. And that Claire, she was a ripe and sweet little vixen. She had no experience, but she was easy on the eyes and Jerry liked easy on the eyes. He'd been staring at Lindsey's wrinkled skin for the last twenty years, but Claire was soft and sweet. That good girl façade only went so far until what lies beneath the surface bubbles over and splits the divide between good girl and the heat of youth.

She'd make a good servant.

Perhaps you should take her as your own.

He clenched his fists even tighter, feeling that pressure across the nape of his neck.

And do away with the old hag.

We must leave no stone unturned. We need **hearts** *for the master.*

28

Carver called the investigation off. The tarps were holding, but that last gale just about swept them into the Hudson. Plus, the storm was relentless, finding every crevice in the tarp and raining across his crime scene. He was grateful they were able to gather as much evidence as they had. Evidence that was on its way to the crime lab to be analyzed, broken down, and reconstructed. The body was taken to the morgue, and Carver had a ton of questions for them. Namely, how was it done? How was the girl's heart ripped out of her chest?

Carver remembered the satanic scare in the eighties. Although he never handled such a situation personally, he had heard of more than a few satanic rituals that occurred across the nation. Plus, the *60 Minutes* special on the topic spread fear like wildfire and had every parent in the nation watching every move their children made. For a while, every murder was linked to a satanic ritual, or, at the very least, Satanism was mentioned as a possible motive, especially when the murder involved a child. Carver knew how many children disappeared every year. Way too many, but they weren't all victims of a satanic ritual, although he was certain some were, considering the stories he'd heard from his fellow policemen.

Now that pentagram burned in his brain. Along with the words Initium Novum.

Humanity's end as a new beginning.

What the fuck does that mean? Obviously, someone's got a gripe with humanity. Carver watched from his Chevrolet as the last officers pulled away from the crime scene. The street was barren; the storm sending every pedestrian indoors. A few cars sloshed through the rain while Carver chewed on a new toothpick. But damn, did he want a cigarette. He could feel that cool menthol in his lungs, bringing calm and ease to his mind. Instead, he gnawed on that thin piece of wood.

No witnesses. No identification, and Carver knew what that meant. He'll be spending his evening sifting through missing persons' files by the truckload, trying to discover exactly who this girl is. Was. And what she was doing in Sleepy Hollow. Someone had to know her. Someone always comes out, looking and hoping to find their loved one, and never considering the dark recesses of sin and murder as a possibility.

Humanity's end as a new beginning.

Does that mean this is the first in what he can expect to be a series of murders? Is there a serial killer in his city? Their eyes roaming over every citizen, watching and waiting, assessing and choosing their next victim. Carver was well aware that murdering pigs enjoy watching their crime scene. Could be doing that very thing right at this moment, watching Carver chewing on his toothpick and sizing him up for a heavyweight title fight between the great detective and the murdering bastard. He looked through his windshield, investigating the apartments surrounding the scene. Looking for suspicious, prying eyes when his CB crackled.

"Detective Carver."

Carver gripped his CB, providing the necessary information to dispatch.

"The medical examiner is ready for you."

Good, I'll finally get some answers.

"Ok, dispatch. I'm on my way."

He replaced his CB and took another look through his windshield.

Humanity's end as a new beginning.

The phrase bothered him, turning his gut into a noxious boil. Something sinister was happening in his city and Carver understood the killer was on the prowl, searching for his next victim. How many more will fall under his thumb? He wasn't certain, but he could hope. Hope he could catch the son of a bitch before the morgue had a full house of victims.

29

"I just have to say, Jerry, I think you're making a mistake."

Lindsey always thought it was necessary to voice her opinion. The woman had no filter and refused to accept her position in life. Some people should just keep their pie hole shut and never speak a word about important matters. Opinions were like assholes. Everyone's got one. She was standing by his desk, looking down at him, holding the paperwork as if she refused to hand it over.

"Selling the property to the first buyer is not a smart decision. The land is worth so much; you're better off fielding multiple offers and letting everyone drive the price up. You're leaving money on the table."

But Jerry never heard a word from the woman. His attention fixed on the paperwork.

"Jerry?" He lifted his eyes to her. "What's wrong with you?"

I'll take the paperwork now.

He stretched his arm towards her. "I'll take the paperwork, thank you."

Lindsey paused, looking him over and chewing on her bottom lip. She shook her head when she handed him the bundle. "It's a damn shame."

Jerry licked his lips as he took the bundle and placed it on his desk. "Send Claire in to notarize."

Lindsey stood for a moment as Jerry combed through the paperwork before she stomped out of his office, telling Claire to join him with her notary stamp. The paperwork was completed with Marc Saduj receiving the property, although no monetary value was assigned. Not yet at least. He'd informed Lindsey that he would add the information himself. The whisper in his ear hadn't divulged the selling price, yet, although Jerry knew it was forthcoming.

He was signing his name on the dotted line when Claire knocked and let herself in. After notarizing, he instructed her to file the necessary paperwork with the city. They'll be closed soon, so she had to hurry. Claire was a good little worker and took off with her assignment like a bat out of hell.

And Jerry sat listening, watching Lindsey bitch and moan as she sat at her desk, reviewing next weeks' meetings and closings and listings and open houses. He chuckled to himself when the thought struck about how mad Lindsey is going to be when she discovers the selling price was one dollar. That chuckle turned into a tightlipped scowl when the voice whispered in his ear.

Maybe it's time we teach the opinionated Lindsey exactly who is in charge here.

30

Carver followed the medical examiner-Dr. Holland-into the morgue.

Dr. Holland is a short and heavyset bulk of a man, with glasses hanging from his thick round nose, large blue eyes, and a mop of dirty blonde hair.

"I've never seen anything like it, detective." Dr. Holland kept walking as he talked, his white coat flapping behind him. "If you ask me, we've got one of those satanic rituals on our hands."

Carver took the toothpick from his lips. "What makes you say that?" Carver had his eyes on the slab they were walking towards. A sheet covered the body beneath.

"Well, considering the nature of the crime and the fact that the heart is missing, concludes this is some sort of ritual killing. Plus, the pentagram is a dead giveaway."

Carver was a little put off with Holland's statement. Information about the crime scene should have been kept under wraps. Carver's police were not supposed to share information with anyone outside the force. Sometimes a police unit was worse than a southern sewing circle, where lives revolved around gossip.

"Or it's a lead to nowhere."

They were standing over the covered body when Carver noticed how quiet it was in the basement. He couldn't even hear the storm raging outside. The fluorescent lights cast a dull bluish glow across the room and Holland's teeth captured those lights. He looked like something from a comic strip.

Holland cocked his head to his right. "What'd you mean?"

"Sometimes, a clue is left as a deterrent to the real crime to get the police to look one way when they need to be looking elsewhere. It's a common theme among murderers. In the eighties, mafia hitmen were using pentagrams to throw the police off to the fact that the murder was a mob hit. I've seen it more than a few times."

Holland just stared at him with a skeptical eye. "Well, let's see what we got." Holland pulled the sheet off the body. The body that had grown pale now captured the dull blue glow. The gaping hole in the girl's chest smelled awful and Carver instinctively turned his head away.

"She's a bit gamey," said Holland. "Do you need some menthol rub?"

Carver shook his head. "Let's just see what you got."

"Very well, detective." He hovered over the body, using his pinky finger to identify what he was referring to, pointing to the side of the hole. "See these indentations? It's not a perfect round hole, as if a tool created the hole."

Carver cocked his head, his eyes squinted. He looked up at Holland. "And?"

"Well, when she first arrived, my first instinct was to identify what tool was used. I was thinking some kind of sharpened or serrated hole cutter… like what they use on golf courses to dig new holes." He looked at Carver as if waiting for him to reply. When he didn't, Holland kept going. "But do you see this here? On the right side are indentations. The only thing I can think of that could make those indentations is a fist." He gripped the sheet and pulled it over her head.

"A fist?"

Holland gave a quick nod, with closed eyes and tight lips. "Correct, detective. As in, whoever did this used their fist to make the hole. Those indentations are from the murderer's knuckles."

Carver paused, thinking. "I was told it would take the strength of ten men to punch a hole through someone's chest."

Holland cocked his head again. "Yes and no, but a very powerful man could do it, especially if he was hopped up on speed. Besides, what other explanation do we have other than something supernatural?"

To this, Carver eyeballed Holland with a sudden jerk of his head. "Supernatural?"

"Yes, detective. Do you not believe in the supernatural?" He looked around the room. "All we get down here is the supernatural. The dead have a way of speaking, detective. You would be wise to heed their warning."

Carver gnawed on his toothpick, transferring it to the corner of his mouth. "Duly noted," he muttered, staring at the sheet and the body beneath it.

"So, perhaps the satanic theory holds a bit of water."

"Maybe, but then again, maybe it's like you said, some muscle head hopped up on speed loses it and then writes the pentagram on the wall as a deterrent."

To this, Dr. Holland grinned. "Either way, detective, that's for you to discover."

"Indeed." Carver rolled his toothpick between his fingertips, staring at the dead body.

"Is that all, detective? I have some work to do with her, and should I find additional information, I'll call the station, but that concludes my preliminary report."

Carver thanked Dr. Holland before returning to his car. There was still no identification on the victim, and now this... someone punched a hole through her chest and ripped out her heart. Maybe it was just a hopped-up muscle head on speed. Or even steroids. Maybe they just lost it in a roid rage and then panicked, writing that pentagram as a result. But how often does a panicked person not make a mistake? He visualized the pentagram in his mind's eye. He could see it dripping down the wall. *If you just killed someone in a panic, how shaky would the hand be while writing that pentagram?* Pretty damn shaky, he was certain, but the pentagram looked like it had been written with a calm hand by someone who had all the time in the world. It just didn't make sense.

Although, if it was true and it was a roid rage, the heart they took would have been a part of the ploy. So where is the heart if it wasn't used in some sick ritual? Maybe it was still in the alley, discarded like yesterday's garbage. Carver looked up to the rain-drenched sky. He'll have to call in a search team. Call in the dogs too.

Hopefully, they'll be able to locate the heart.

31

The phone rang, startling Marc and he jumped in his chair, spilling his scotch across his lap.

"Fuck," he groaned, immediately wiping his pants. He placed his glass on the table and brushed his pants a few more times. He was on his fourth glass for the evening and had been nipping at his fingernails for the better part of the last hour. His head buzzed with alcohol. Alcohol that allowed the tears to fall without shame while watching the rain and listening to the thunder roar above his building. On the fourth ring, he answered the call.

"Hello." His voice was low and guttural. He was hoping to mask his intoxication. He cleared his throat, that buzz in his skull growing and thickening as he waited with bated breath for the person to answer. He squeezed the receiver. He could hear it crunch inside his hand.

Silence.

"Hello?"

He could hear movement on the other end. With the tension building in his chest, he could barely breathe.

"Marc?" The voice came through. Marc recognized it immediately. The nurse had a distinct voice.

Marc pursed his lips and cleared his throat again. "Yes, it's Marc."

She seemed to settle down. "Good, it's Jessica, the…"

"Yes, I know. I recognized your voice. Thank you for returning the call."

Silence. A pause.

"Jessica?"

"Yes, I'm here. I wasn't aware you called."

Marc's gut twisted that nausea to his brain, the scotch souring in his stomach. If she wasn't returning his call, then what prompted the current phone call?

"I did. A few hours ago."

"Sorry. I've been busy with patients."

Marc breathed deeply, closing his eyes and squeezing the receiver. "Is there an update on Lori?" His voice cracked with the word *update*. Then silence, but Marc could hear a car humming over the road, commotion, and talking.

"Is everything okay?" Marc waited for an answer.

"I'm calling from a payphone outside the hospital. My shift is over." She paused, as if waiting for prying ears to leave. "I don't feel safe calling you from the ICU. She's watching and listening to everything. That Elena is something else."

Marc said nothing. All he wanted was an update. He couldn't care less about Elena. The storm raged outside. Howling winds and thunder, lightning. Raindrops thundered against his windows. He could hear a truck's brakes squeal over the receiver.

"Is there an update on Lori?"

"Elena's assessing. Lori is scheduled for another surgery tomorrow to relieve the pressure on her brain. But the bleeding hasn't stopped and if she can't pull through, Elena indicated she would take her off life support on Monday. At least we were able to take her tube out, so that's a good thing." And she paused again as Marc's heart sank into his stomach with a hollowed out painful sting. "I can get in a lot of trouble for telling you this, but I felt it was necessary. But that's all I can say right now, Marc. You'll have to sit tight and hope and pray for the best, but whatever you do, don't come to the hospital. Your picture has been shared with security and if you show up, you'll be arrested. Elena saw you leaving the ICU this morning. She was hell to deal with. It's not worth it, Marc. You won't even make it to the ICU.... It's a damn shame what money can do."

He paused and felt the world spin. Tightness in his chest. Hard to breathe, and that scotch boiled into his brain.

"I'm off tomorrow, but I'll be in on Monday and will update you then."

Marc's voice arrived like a whiny child lost in the dark recesses of the night. "What am I supposed to do if I can't come there? I need to be there."

"After you left this morning, Elena had a blowout with the hospital administrator. She's paying for additional security. There's no way you'll make it to her room, and then you'll be sitting in a jail cell and losing your mind without knowing what's going on with Lori. It's best to stay put and wait."

"That'll drive me insane." He shook his head and gritted his teeth, frustrated, his anger boiling beneath the surface.

Noticed his scar started itching again. He rubbed it furiously.

"It is what it is, Marc. Please don't tell anyone I called you. I've got a child to worry about, and I need this job." Another pause and then, "I've got to go. Listen, take care of yourself and try to stay distracted. I'll call you on Monday." And she hung up, leaving Marc holding the receiver as her words settled in his mind.

A single tear fell from his left eye.

Thwack!

Marc snapped his head around to his front door. His eyes narrowed when a shadow waved beneath the bottom gap. Then shuffling when the phone started beeping in thick and quick successions. He hung up the phone and heard that shuffling again. Like fabric against the door. The shadow moved again as if someone was behind the door, swaying back and forth. Thunder rolled with a sonic boom, quaking the building. Lightning drenched his apartment in a blue cosmic glow, then disappeared. Marc realized how dark his apartment was. The shadow beneath the door was blocking the hall light from beaming through the crevice on his front door.

Someone was outside his apartment, listening. His scar itched something awful, and he pressed against it, hard, hoping to relieve the itch. He stood up and stared at his front door, listening to the shuffling while watching the shadow wave back and forth.

Marc took cautious steps to the foyer, being sure not to make a sound, staring at the bottom of the door, watching the shadow. He took a step closer, staring at the peephole where he could see the hall light. There were no shadows floating past his peephole, so he stepped forward and looked through it.

The hall was barren. He unlatched the deadbolt and swung the door open. His attention caught by the inverted pentagram on his door. In the center of the pentagram were the words, Initium Novum. All painted in red.

"What the…"

He stepped into the hall to the stairs. No one was on the steps. No shuffling or footsteps tapping the concrete. No voice and no noise. Silence greeted him within the howling wind and rain. He looked back at his door. He'll need to clean that up as soon as possible. The last thing he needed was a vandal causing him trouble. *How the hell did they get in here?* More than likely Mrs. Leiter had a vandal in the building, considering the only way through the front door was either a key or buzzed entry from someone inside. He'll be lodging his complaint immediately.

But first, he required another drink.

32

Claire had never been prouder. She successfully arrived at the courthouse before closing, registering the documents Jerry had signed with the county and city. She couldn't wait to tell Jerry.

She parked outside the office and noticed all the lights were off, although Lindsey's and Jerry's cars were still parked outside.

Perhaps the lights went out because of the storm?

She waited in her car; the storm was dropping buckets of rain across the parking lot. Thunder rolled overhead and lightning speared across the sky, followed by a howl of wind.

"Jesus, is this a bad storm."

She cut off the radio-Eddie Vedder had been singing about a *Red Mosquito*-and allowed the storm to take center stage. The parking lot was flooded. She'll be soaked by the time she gets to the front door. Wished she'd brought a pair of boots instead of high heels, but the weatherman never said anything about rain today. Damn weather people never get anything right. She looked at the sky with the hope that the storm would soon subside. Thunder cracked and the rain fell in heavier sheets.

Maybe not.

She laughed at herself. Laughed because there was nothing left to do but get soaked to the bone. She has plans tonight-time out with the girls-and if she's going to make it on time she needs to get out of work on time and considering her shift ended ten minutes ago she needed to get the hell out of Dodge and be done with her weekend duties. She cut off the engine and grabbed the plastic file folder from the front seat where the registered documents, including the receipt for filing the documents, were. She dropped her keys in her pocket and jumped out of the car into the rain. Less than a second out of the car and she was already drenched. Her feet cold and wet, she was standing in a forever puddle in the parking lot that reached her ankles, even with the damn high heels.

Claire ducked her head and trekked across the parking lot, holding the plastic folder close to her chest. The front door in her line of sight. Rain battered her with a relentless fury. More thunder. More lightning. Howling winds forced raindrops into her eyes. Her feet sloshed through the rain. She arrived at the front door and swung it open, stepping inside with a hurried step and closing the door quickly.

She stood against the glass door, breathing heavy, wet and huffing. Staring. It was so quiet in the office. Quiet to the point that she thought she was alone. The lights were off, but there was no Lindsey or Jerry to greet her. She looked at Jerry's office and noticed the lights were off in there too, and the blinds had been shuttered. A thump came from the back room and Claire immediately turned in that direction. But then silence. Her eyes narrow, her chest tight, her arms too, clutching the file folder like a lifeline.

"Hello. Mr. Hardwood? Lindsey?" Her voice lost power when she said Lindsey.

Silence. Nothing but the slow steady breath rising and falling in her lungs. And the rain, of course, the rain that dropped sheets across the building. Claire pursed her lips and swallowed her breath.

She checked the time-there was a clock on the wall to her right-and understood she needed to get and go and leave if she was going to make it on time. Claire stepped across the waiting room to the receptionist's desk, walking behind it when she dropped the file folder on the desk, pulled the seat back, and sat down. She took a pen from a cup holder and a notepad. She'll write Jerry a note and leave the folder on his desk along with the note explaining that she had plans and had to leave.

Maybe there was more to the relationship between Lindsey and Jerry than Claire knew. Perhaps-she concluded-that bump she heard was the two of them. Sure, Lindsey is old enough to be Jerry's mother, but does that really matter? Claire understood that everyone had needs and if the old lady was getting a little on the side from a younger man, so be it. She took a napkin and blotted her wet hands before writing the note then zipped that pen across the paper, gathered the file folder and took the note to Jerry's office, her attention caught by the cold rasp that filtered down the hallway to her ears.

Like a whisper caught between dimensions. As if someone was standing in the hall and watching her every move, whispering from the netherworld. She could feel the presence in the hall, thick and profound, paralyzing every limb in her body, constricting the heart and lungs with an impression wrought with fear.

But then again, there was no one there, and Claire cursed herself for foolish intuition. She could hear the air in the hall, as if it was forced through a funnel to her ears.

Initium Novum.

Claire repeated the same, under her breath, her own whisper. Her breath caught in her throat. She swallowed it down, then gripped the doorknob and opened Jerry's door, then froze. Staring. Her head bent.

The office was dark; the only light came from the darkened and gray sky outside that dropped rain across the parking lot. But she could see it, the inverted pentagram drawn on Jerry's wall. The words, Initium Novum, written in red beneath the pentagram. And the letters were dripping, cascading down the wall. She followed the stream to the body lying across the credenza that looked like a ghost. The skin was so pale, the body beamed in the darkness like pale death. At first, she thought it was a trick, refusing to believe what she was looking at, but when the lightning cast its blue glow through the room, she knew it was Lindsey.

She'd been cut open from her throat to her navel, her innards draped like dead snakes frozen in time from her cut torso to the floor. They looked like spider legs and if Lindsey had risen at that very moment and walked on those spider legs, Claire would not have been surprised. But she didn't. Couldn't because she was dead. Dead, but her eyes were staring, illuminated by lightning. Staring at Claire through dead, black eyeballs.

She told herself to run. To get the hell out and call the police, but her feet refused to follow her thought. She closed her eyes when the nape of her neck cringed, her breath caught in her throat. Something cold brushed across her neck. Claire reluctantly turned, inching her head around.

She stepped back when she saw Jerry. His eyes were black, as if madness had surfaced in his eyeballs. She could see her reflection in those black mirrors. Saw how frightened she was, how startled and fearful. There was blood on Jerry's skin, across his cheeks and mouth. He used his arm to wipe his lips, his arm pale and moist with perspiration as he gasped with a breath down his throat and smeared that blood across his face.

"Initium Novum." Jerry's words came off his lip's monotone, as if he were repeating a phrase that was spoken to him. "Humanity's end as a new beginning."

Claire's jaw dropped. She could feel his presence, large and barreling on top of her. Hard to move. Difficult to breathe. She willed herself to say something. Anything. Placate the man so she can leave. Play nice, but she never got the words out. Jerry stepped forward with the speed of a cat and had his hands wrapped around her throat before she could even blink.

That file folder dropped to the ground, kicked by Jerry himself. It skid to a stop beneath the credenza. Jerry laughed like a buffoon, thick and hearty as he strangled the air from her lungs.

Black spots formed in her vision, his fingers so tight across her windpipe, her eyeballs bulged from their sockets. Jerry rang Claire's neck as if she were a rag doll, his strength inhuman. Claire slapped and clawed his face, desperate to live.

Although Claire knew all too well. There was no way she was meeting the girls tonight.

Jessica, the nurse, was right. Marc needed to distract himself. His thoughts kept looping and bouncing across his skull. He was scrubbing the pentagram off his door. Trying to, at least, but all he managed to do was smear the paint. Sure, he accomplished fading the red paint but there were still streaks of red across the door. Although no one will be able to tell that the red paint used to form a pentagram, he could still see the red, streaked in thin lines as if it had always been a part of the door.

He thought about Lori while mindlessly scrubbing and swathing and scrubbing some more.

"Additional security?" He shook his head, pausing with the scrub brush in his hand. "Fucking Elena." He could feel the tears threatening but refused to allow them to fall; he sucked them back with a snort through his nose.

He pushed on his scar. All he could feel was that itch bubbling into his left eyeball, turning it red and burning and watering. Felt like his eyeball was going to burst. His vision blurred every time he pushed on his scar. He picked up his drink-the glass next to him on the floor beside his knees-and sipped furiously. The scotch helped numb the itch and burning. He savored the scotch on his tongue and between his cheeks as he put his glass down, then swallowed hard, staring at his door with a gasp, his mouth burning.

Felt that hot scotch in his stomach, drowning his intestines. Felt like there was a pool of scotch swimming in his gut.

He stared, crooked at the door. Red paint was scoured in semicircles across the wood. No matter how hard he scrubbed, he couldn't get it all off. The water in the bucket was dark with red and beige mixed with the dirt and dust from his door. Some of the beige paint on the door had come off, revealing the bone-white color beneath it. Satisfied-well, as satisfied as much as he cared about the door-Marc dropped the scrub brush into his bucket, then gathered his glass and the bucket, and brought them to the kitchen counter. He looked at the bottle of scotch on the counter, his head heavy and his mind swimming in alcohol.

"Lori?" he whispered.

You'll be arrested on sight. They have your picture. You'll never make it to the ICU. It's best to distract yourself.

He gripped the bottle, his hands trembling. Squeezed the top off and poured, missing the glass completely on the first try. He filled the glass then, up to the brim, emptying the bottle. Thunder raged over the Hudson. The storm was passing now, moving across the river, dwindling to a steady light rain. Night had fallen over his city; he could see the full moon banishing clouds from its view. The dark clouds slithered across the moon to places unknown.

How many times had he been in this very spot staring at the moon? He'd lived in the apartment for most of his life, but why he moved back after his father's passing, he did not know. There was nothing but nightmares in the apartment. So many malicious ghosts from the past who refused to die. It was the view, the view he was looking at now, that offered inspiration any writer could muse over. The view drew him back to the apartment like gravity.

He never thought about the nightmares, memories, or ghosts. Never returned to the past or the day his mother died. Jesus, if he ever told Lori the truth about that day, she would never agree to stay in the apartment. But Marc had to. He had to come to terms with the past to enhance the future.

"What fucking future?"

He sipped his scotch, savoring the hot fluid on his tongue. His eyes were wet with tears. His head was numb and buzzing and the itch. Of course, the itch was there.

Icy breath on the nape of his neck. He cringed as the hair on his neck stood erect, shivering down his spine. He turned to the open door. Nothing. The hall was empty, but he could feel it; a presence in the hall, thick and cold, and Marc knew the man in black was watching him.

"Are you satisfied?" Marc's voice was hoarse, his throat dry. "This is what you want, isn't it? Always in the shadows, taking everything from me." He wavered and stepped back, catching himself before falling. Felt pressure on his chest, like energetic fingers attempting to push him over. "Get away from me!" He pushed back, losing his balance. His glass crashed against the wall, shattering into a million pieces across the stove, counter and floor, spilling scotch everywhere.

"I told you a long time ago to leave me… a…fucking… *looooooone!*"

A light flickered from down the hall, and then the smell arrived. That dank profound scent, so rank and foul, of burning baking soda and cocaine. The smoke slithered like Satan's breath down the hall. He could hear the man in black laugh as Marc closed his eyes. The scent was everywhere, invading his nostrils and boiling acid into the back of his throat. Thunder rumbled in the distance with a sudden flash of lightning as Marc opened his eyes. The hall light flickered on and off. On and off. On and off.

And he could hear and feel the breath, the presence of the man in black standing in the foyer floated to the hall towards the master bedroom. Marc stepped into the foyer, staring into the empty hall past the front door, then back to the apartment's hallway. The dark hall turned bright when the light from the master bedroom turned on. Then off again. Calling him. Willing him to the bedroom.

"Marc baby, come here." His mother's voice. "Please, Marc, momma *neeeeds* you." He pursed his lips and swallowed the lump in his throat. "Come to me."

He closed his eyes as he gritted his teeth and when he opened them, his dad was standing in the doorway to the master bedroom, dressed in the same suit Marc buried him in. The suit was dark gray and glued to his thick frame. Clean shaven and his hair was like a carpeted fuzz across his balding head. He stepped into the room and disappeared when the light in the bedroom returned.

"Please, Marc. Momma needs you." His mother's voice was whiny with a dramatic drawl.

He stepped towards the hall, his gait unsteady. Felt like he was walking sideways, the floor shifting beneath his feet. Picture frames occupied the hall wall. Pictures that had been on the wall for decades. Family pictures that now all hung crooked, as if the man in black had tipped them over on his way to the bedroom. Marc's fifth birthday. The family trip to Florida. Marc's fifth grade graduation. The family portrait and Marc's grade school pictures, and in every single one of them, over Marc's shoulder, was the man in black. The bedroom light flickered off once again, bathing the hall in shadow. He could feel the energy filtering from the bedroom into the hall. Thick and unrelenting, like a black hole existed on the other side of the doorway, pulling him closer. That rank stench of crack cocaine thickened in the hall.

"Come to me."

Marc stepped into the doorway. His mother was sitting up on the bed leaning against the headboard. A glass pipe sat on the comforter, her drink on the side table. Her blonde hair, greasy and nappy, fell to her shoulders. Her dark pink and silk spaghetti-strapped nightgown clung to her sweaty skin. She was staring at her wrists. Her bleeding wrists. With tears in her eyes, she coddled her hands close to her chest then turned to Marc. Her frosted blue eyes wet with tears.

"I'm sorry, mom." He turned away. "Sorry for what I did."

"You cut me good," she said. "Never saw it coming." Her voice subtle and defeated, she closed her eyes and held those wrists tight against her chest. "Death," she said, turning and staring at him. "Is worse than life could ever be."

Marc squeezed across his lips, "If I could take it back, I would."

"You've always been a nasty, useless child. Now you're a worthless adult. Can't even get into the hospital to see Lori. What good are you?"

"I'm sorry for who I am." He pushed on his scar, wanting to rip his head off.

"Sorry won't cut it, Marc. You owe us so much more. You owe us your heart and soul."

"What do you want me to do?"

"The man in black is waiting for you at your father's grave. He has the key to Lori's fate. It will be best to give him what he wants. In order to save Lori, you must give yourself to him."

A shuffling came from the apartment. Marc turned to see his father standing in the front doorway. He stepped into the hall towards the stairs and vanished.

"Go to your father. The man in black waits for you there." Her voice was a whisper in his ear.

And when he turned, he was alone. Alone and in the dark.

Listening to the distant rumble of thunder.

34

Carver was watching the dogs, sniffing and trotting down the alley, looking for the heart. He was grateful the storm subsided, although he hoped that if the heart was in the alley, the rain didn't wash away the scent.

Judging by the dogs, he was certain they would locate the heart without a problem. If it was still here.

Someone punched a hole through her chest.

"Poor child." Carver rolled his toothpick into the corner of his mouth. "Who did this to you? Talk to me, please."

As if the dead could talk.

"Detective?"

Carver turned to the flatfoot walking towards him.

"I just heard from dispatch. They've been trying to reach you."

"I'll check in once the search is completed. There's nothing to report at this…"

"That's not what they want."

Carver perked up. "What happened, officer?"

"We got an ID on the victim." He paused. "Well, there's a lead at least…" He hesitated and Carver waited for him to collect himself. The officer pulled a small notebook from his front pocket, flipped the cover, and scanned what was written. "A mother called in a missing person's report about an hour ago with a description matching the victim. She said her daughter spent the night at a friend's house and was supposed to be home by noon but never returned. The description she gave matches the victim to a tee."

"I'll be damned," said Carver, rolling that toothpick from one side of his mouth to the other. "Anything else?"

"Yes, there is." The officer cleared his throat. "The husband is missing, too. She said he was supposed to be home hours ago, but she hadn't heard from him, and she said that's not like him at all. She even tried calling his office but got no response. Not even from the receptionist. She said everything's gone dark. Her words, not mine."

Carver looked at the dogs, still sniffing and scouring across the alley. "Did she provide an address for the office?"

"Sure did."

"Good, radio dispatch and have them send a black and white to see what's going on over there."

"Yes, sir. Consider it done."

Carver paused, thinking. Thinking about the mother and, if it is her daughter whose heart was ripped out of her chest, how he'll have to deliver some very bad news. He hoped he could locate the husband. She'll need him now more than ever.

"Anything else, sir?"

Carver looked at the officer. "Tell dispatch I'll roll by the mother's house after the search is completed, which should be soon. It doesn't look like we're going to find anything tonight."

"Sir, yes, sir."

"Get it done, officer."

Carver turned to the dogs once again, eager to have the search completed as the young flatfoot took the radio from his hip. He was about to speak when Carver asked, "What is the name of the family?"

The officer's jaw hung loose, the radio crackling in his ear while he scanned his notebook. "Hardwood, sir. Business is Hardwood Realty."

And Carver said, "Jerry?"

35

Officer Frankenberri pulled his black and white into the small parking lot of Hardwood Realty. The office was dark, not one light could be seen from the street. It looked dead to him. Cold and dead, and if it hadn't been for the three cars parked outside, he would have left without a second pause.

On the drive over, Frankenberri received another call from dispatch. Apparently, a mother had called, concerned about her daughter, Claire. She was supposed to be home a few hours ago but never arrived, and she wasn't answering her cell phone either, which sent up a few red flags for the mother. The daughter was also employed by Hardwood Realty. So, that's two Hardwood Realty employees who were on the missing person's watch. Frankenberri shined the floodlight attached to his side mirror across the cars, focusing on the license plates. He confirmed one of the three cars belonged to Jerry Hardwood and another to Claire Randolph, the same two missing persons. The third he was unsure about, but he provided the necessary information to dispatch to receive an identification on the owner.

Frankenberri clucked his tongue, staring at the cold and dark office. He informed dispatch he was going to the front door before he climbed out of his black and white. The air was cool and moist against his skin, grateful the storm had passed. He kept the floodlight on as he approached. It looked quiet inside. The light illuminated the front of the office. A waiting area followed by a receptionist's desk were barren and unoccupied. He could see an office on his right and a hall that stretched past the reception desk into the back of the office. Officer Frankenberri rapped on the glass door, then waited, craning his neck to see further into the office, down the hall. He tried the door handle. Unlocked. He looked toward the hall. Nothing. Just dark and empty and…

Perhaps someone is in there… Bleeding to death. Perhaps they need officer assistance.

The whisper was cold against his ear and Frankenberri wondered if that was his thought or some instinct willing him to go inside. Two missing people, both tracked to the same location. Both with cars in the parking lot. Maybe there's some strange sex stuff happening in the office. Some ménage à trois and wouldn't that be something special to walk in on. He rapped on the door again.

"Hello," he called, "Sleepy Hollow PD. I'm coming in."

Frankenberri entered the office and immediately noticed how hot it was, muggy and thick with heat. He turned around to the floodlight that beamed into his eyes, just to be certain no one was behind him. He radioed dispatch, informing them he had entered the office and received the common cautionary verbiage in return.

"Hello. Sleepy Hollow PD." He pursed his lips and swallowed. "Claire? Mr. Hardwood? Are you here?"

A shift behind the office door, as if someone was shuffling to the door or jumped off a desk or chair. Or someone was dragging something across the floor. Frankenberri went to the office, his hand on his holstered revolver.

He gripped the doorknob. "Mr. Hardwood? Are you in there?" He opened the door, and it creaked open. His jaw dropped at the sight, eyes wide and staring. An inverted pentagram occupied the far wall, the words Initium Novum written in blood, blood that dripped down the wall to the dead body on the credenza. He pulled his revolver and stepped into the office and almost tripped over the body lying on the floor.

"My God," he whispered. "What is this?"

The girl lying on the floor was young. She had hand marks around her throat, and her eyes bulged from their sockets. Her skin was ghostly pale. Frankenberri knelt and checked for a pulse, her skin cold and stiff. No pulse. Frankenberri looked past the door into the waiting area. Nothing behind him. He trampled over to the body on the credenza, but he didn't have to check that pulse. The woman was gutted, and her innards were draped from her body to the ground. She had a gaping hole in her chest too, and Frankenberri turned with a cringe when he looked inside. There was no heart in the body. Gritting his teeth, he unclipped his radio and immediately called in his report, requesting immediate assistance when he heard the wet slopping and hearty grinning chewing coming from the office corner, behind the door.

Frankenberri dropped his radio on the desk and held his revolver with both hands.

"Come out from behind the door. This is the Sleepy Hollow police." His voice was nervous and choked back-now that he'd seen the rotting open corpse, the stench was in full bloom, and he did all he could to stuff down the puke that burned in the back of his throat.

But the only response he received was a giddy laugh, like a child chewing on their favorite candy-cheeks full, with a wide grin across their lips.

"I said come out from behind the door."

For the briefest second there was a pause, as if whoever was behind the door had heard him but paid his direction no mind. The chewing and giddy laughter started up again and Frankenberri shuffled to the door. He couldn't see much of anything. The blinds were closed and not even his floodlight could penetrate the darkness in the room, although the floodlight shed shadows across the wall through the shuttered blinds.

Frankenberri pursed his lips and swallowed. He tried again, "Sleepy Hollow PD, come out from behind the door."

More giddy laughter. Laughter in the darkness behind the door. Frankenberri shuffled closer. Reached his hand out and swung the door open and stepped back.

The man-Frankenberri made a snap judgment that it was Jerry Hardwood-was crouched behind the door, eating with a big smile across his lips and that laughter, that childlike laughter in his throat. Frankenberri was certain he located the missing heart. It was in Jerry's hands. Some of it, at least. Frankenberri was convinced the rest was between Jerry's teeth or in his stomach. His lips were covered in blood. Frankenberri ordered him to put his hands up and to lie on his stomach, but all he received was a stare that turned his gut and heightened his instincts that danger was on the prowl. That giddy laughter turned to rage in an instant, and Frankenberri saw his reflection in Jerry's dark black eyes.

"The master needs hearts," said Jerry in a groveling, guttural, and seething voice as heart chunks jumped off his lips.

"Mister," Frankenberri said, shaking his head. "I couldn't give a fuck what your master wants, put your hands up and…"

Jerry jumped at him; his hands stretched as if he meant to strangle the officer. Jumped, and the startled Frankenberri squeezed the trigger, plugging Jerry with two bullets that ripped through his chest and dropped him to the floor.

Now the distant sound of approaching sirens rang through Frankenberri's ears. He holstered his weapon and knelt beside the writhing Jerry, his hand over the bullet holes, hoping to stop the bleeding.

"They're coming Jerry. Just hold on."

Wet gurgles in Jerry's throat. "The master needs hearts," he groveled.

Frankenberri looked at the window. The sirens were louder now. He could hear tires screeching to a halt outside the office, the red and blue lights trolling between the blinds.

Jerry said, "I got him one. One heart for the master."

And when Frankenberri looked at him, Jerry was once again smiling, laughing like a giddy child.

36

Sleepy Hollow Cemetery is one of Sleepy Hollow's most visited tourist sites. Founded in 1849, there are over ninety thousand graves across more than 90 acres of cemetery land, flanked by a large arboretum, including maple, locust, spruce, cedar, pine, and oak trees, to name a few. The cemetery serves as the final resting place for many famous writers, philanthropists and scientists including Rockefeller, Astor, Carnegie, Thoreau, and of course, the legend himself, Washington Irving. Just across the street, at the Old Dutch Church of Sleepy Hollow, is where the Headless Horseman had his infamous battle with Ichabod Crane.

The cemetery also serves as the final resting place for Marc's father, Jonathon. Marc felt mesmerized during the walk over. Paranoid too, especially with the entourage of police cars, dogs, and policemen who littered the street the moment he entered Sleepy Hollow. Marc bypassed the police through the side streets, which wasn't a problem for Marc. Considering current circumstances, he was eager to avoid the bar where his mother used to spend her nights. Those memories were best kept at bay. He arrived at the cemetery and had to scale the wall. Apparently, the cemetery refused to allow loved ones to enter after dark, but Marc knew how to enter. He'd been scaling the cemetery walls since he was twelve, mostly to drop acid and spend a trip with the dead.

But tonight was different. The man in black was waiting for him. Marc knew he could help Lori, but what would he have to give in return? It didn't matter, not to Marc. He would do whatever was necessary to raise Lori from the stranglehold of death.

He dropped off the stone wall to the cemetery ground where his sneakers found mud and slick grass. Thunder roared in the distance. The storm was far away, but the clouds remained, slithering across the full moon as if the moon fought with them for a front-row seat to Marc's show. The wind whispered a howl through the trees that dripped the last remnants of rain from their leaves. The air was cool and crisp against his skin. He could feel the coming of autumn in his bones.

Marc stood still, scanning across the wide cemetery with its rolling hills, grave markers, mausoleums, and multiple paths that snaked across the grounds littered with trees and foliage. A cold and white-gray fog slithered between the headstones and trees. Marc stood for a long while, investigating the cemetery, waiting and willing the man in black to find him. But the cemetery was quiet, quiet and still, placating Marc and his fears when a sudden screech sliced through the night.

The owl with its large round eyes was perched on an oak tree, as if guarding the cemetery. Its beak gaped open, and its wings stretched as if to be threatening as the owl hissed at Marc before it dove off the tree and glided across the cemetery into the fog and places unknown. Marc swallowed his breath, his mind swimming in scotch, his stomach boiling with acid. He took a step forward.

Then another, beginning his trek to his father's grave, the fog thickening the further into the cemetery he traveled. Like a dark and foreboding thickness that tainted his blood with poison, the energy wrapped around him like an iron vise and refused to let go.

"Okay, asshole… let's see what you got for me."

His thoughts returned to Lori, unconscious in a hospital bed. The image was a stain on the back of his mind. Lori with her eyes closed, and a bandage wrapped around her head. He squeezed his trembling hands into fists while gritting his teeth, his scar itching and burning and pulsing across his skull. Lori would do it for him, make this trek through the cemetery, if she had to, if she was told it would help him. Lori, who was the best of all people, required supernatural help. He was confident the man in black will oblige his request.

Marc had a twenty-minute walk ahead of him, up and down the rolling hills, further into the western part of the cemetery where his father was waiting.

And the man in black was waiting too.

37

Carver stood outside Hardwood Realty, watching the chaos. Officers and paramedics rushed in and out of the building. A swarm of patrol cars-all with their lights on-occupied the parking lot and led out into the street, flanked by ambulances. Carver had to park on the street and walk to the building, albeit with a hurried step.

Paramedics were wheeling Jerry Hardwood to the ambulance when Carver first arrived. Carver had known Jerry for the better part of three decades and no matter what the scene looked like, Carver knew that Jerry was no murdering son of a bitch. At least not this cold and calculated. There would have been signs pointing to psychopathic tendencies. Caver had never seen one. None of this made sense. And then there was the whole daughter with her heart ripped out situation. The victim was now properly identified by Jerry's wife, Sheila. All roads led to Hardwood Realty and considering the first officer on the scene had stepped into a bloodbath, Jerry was the only living witness outside of law enforcement.

"He was eating her heart."

That's what the flatfoot reported. Jerry was eating his assistant's heart, a woman Jerry had known since he was a young tike running around without a care in the world. Now she was gutted like a pig and her heart ripped out and then eaten. Eaten by

Jerry himself. Jerry, who took two bullets to the torso by the flatfoot who first arrived on the scene.

Jerry was still alive though, and when the paramedics wheeled him outside, Carver could barely get one word in. All Jerry did was laugh and kept repeating,

"The master needs hearts. The master needs hearts in hell."

Carver had stopped the paramedics, an action that caused Jerry to pause. His eyes were wide and staring, investigating Carver as if he'd never laid eyes on him before.

"Jerry, what the hell happened in there?"

To which Jerry responded by burying his head in his shoulder, looking away. "The master needs hearts," he said as he turned back to Carver. A big grin across his lips. "And I got him one." He burst into giddy laughter. Carver noticed the bandage around Jerry's upper torso, wrapped tight with two spots of blood stained across the bandage.

"We've got to get him to the hospital," said one paramedic.

Carver gnawed on his toothpick, staring at Jerry. Jerry and his wide and staring dark eyes. They seemed like dark pits leading to hell as he laughed and guffawed and whined, "The master needs hearts in hell."

Carver gestured for the paramedics to return to their business. He'll have plenty of time to question Jerry about what happened today. The fact that Jerry was responsible for murdering his own daughter was a conclusion that didn't sit well with Carver. Didn't sit well at all. Something wasn't adding up. All this in-your-face type of murder just didn't make sense. Did Jerry just go off the rail and turn psycho overnight?

Carver rolled his toothpick into the corner of his mouth and stepped into Hardwood Realty. Stepped in and braced himself for the gruesome scene he was about to witness.

38

Marc's father waited for him by his gravesite. Marc had stepped up a small hill and, low and behold, his father was there. Marc felt like a man possessed, but he's been here before, when the hallucinations were in full bloom. He remembered, as he stared at the ghost of his father, how the doctor said a head injury could bring back the hallucinations and delusions. But what Marc always knew was that they weren't hallucinations. The doctors had it all wrong. Sometimes a human being can see what others can't.

And Marc was one of them.

He stood, unmoving, staring at his father, whose body was pulsing with light. Jonathon looked the same as he did the day he passed. With one exception, his eyes were all black. Like black pits leading to hell. Looking. Staring at Marc and waiting. Waiting for Marc. Marc who swallowed the lump in his throat before he stepped towards the grave. His father stepped to the headstone and vanished when Marc stopped cold, sensing how the energy from his ghost father dissipated with his image. The cemetery felt empty then, cold and empty as Marc pushed on his scar, gritting his teeth.

A hiss from above and Marc snapped his head to it. That same owl from before-Marc was certain of it-screeched and hissed at him, its beak agape with its wings outstretched, and the full moon beaming bright behind it.

Movement in the corner of his eye. Marc snapped his focus to the grave, his father's grave, noticing a thick stream of fog slithering across the headstone. He felt the energy bump and the heat grow. He stepped closer, forgetting the owl, his feet squishing in the mud and wet grass, trampling to the grave and stopped, not wanting to disturb his father's final resting place. He looked around and saw nothing. Nothing but trees and clouds and hills and graves.

And no man in black.

Laughter. Starting low and then growing. Rising until it reached the full moon above. Laughter on his right and laughter in between the trees on his left. Marc felt like his head was on a swivel, following that laugh across the cemetery. Where did it come from? The man in black was here. Without a doubt, he was here. Marc could tell his laugh, even if it had been a thousand years since he last heard it.

"Where are you?" Marc raised his voice, frustrated. He didn't have time for games and what he knew most was that the man in black enjoyed playing games. The laughter ceased as if whatever throat it emanated from had been cut. And then the energy, like a thick pulsing that pressed into Marc's flesh, infecting his cells, ballooned off the gravesite.

The owl screeched as a roll of thunder rumbled in the distance. Wind lifted off the ground, breezing across Marc's skin, nagging that itch from his scar. He looked down at the grave and the swirling leaves skittering across the unkempt ground. It felt like electricity. A monster of energy rising from the grave. Marc reached his hand out, his fingers slightly raised, feeling how the air had grown thick and hot, as thick fog-smoke rippled from the ground, swirling into the air, stopping eye level with Marc. He could see red eyes in the fog, drifting, swirling. And the fog grinned as if it were alive. Alive with eyes and lips and teeth.

Then the whispers Marc had been waiting for arrived in a comfortable state of nostalgia.

Come to me. Enter the parallel. I wait for you there.

Electric arcs flitted across Marc's fingers, and he gritted his teeth, glaring at the fog. His scar was itching like a madman hopped up on heroin when he stepped in. Stepped in and felt the fog swallow him whole.

Stepped in and the world turned upside down.

39

Wren finished consuming the heart when he felt the room buzz with an energy he found magnificent. And with it he knew, he knew Marc had entered the parallel, the place his master referred to as the prison that held him at bay, unable to cross into the realm of flesh and bone, always just out of reach. Doomed to live like a ghost, an electrical wave with a conscious thought.

Initium Novum. My master will be here soon.

Wren despised humanity. He wished to see it destroyed and for every human to beg for death. A death he would happily oblige, but even their afterlife would be torture. There will be no escaping from the hand of his master. All they've been planning has now come to fruition. Every piece to their puzzle strategically placed in what has taken more than a century to accomplish. Every whisper and every manipulation contrived from the darkest mind with the single purpose to unleash hell across humanity and bathe the human race in tyranny, blood, and darkness. To turn the heart of love into pure wretched evil.

He sat on the floor, cross-legged, in the basement. He hadn't left since Jerry took leave. He ran his arm across his mouth, smearing blood onto his sleeve. Consuming the girl's heart felt like pure ecstasy. The master needs hearts. With every heart consumed in his honor, the master grew stronger. And Wren was all too willing to devour every heart he could. He looked up, up to the vaulted ceiling, listening. The storm had passed and what a whirlwind it had been, dropping chaos across Sleepy Hollow. His gaze shifted to the bottle of Absinthe standing tall, close to him. Wren reached for it and cradled the bottle close to his chest.

The changing liquid was in the bottle, cursed by the devil himself. Did he dare to drink from the bottle? His mouth salivated at the thought, but the master would not permit it. Such indulgence leads to scattered minds and Wren required a clear head. *This is not the end*, Wren thought to himself.

"It is the beginning… of the end."

He laughed and clucked his tongue.

"The end of humanity."

But what Wren knew above all is that the master will need to take more lives if he's to become flesh and bone.

And Wren was ready to unleash hell on Sleepy Hollow.

40

All he could hear was the steady whack of a hammer. When Marc first entered the fog, he had felt weightless, but now, in the aftermath of the fog energy, he felt heavy, as if his bones had become dense and thickened upon his entrance.

He was still in the cemetery, but this was different. Like a world existing on top of and in-between the world Marc knew. Everything was slanted and oblong, as if the world around him was stretched and contorted by the hands of the devil. A red film, a tint reflective of fire and burning, covered the cemetery as if all the headstones were being cooked over hot coals. The trees looked dead and were covered in a thick black film, as if death had captured them in its cold embrace. Their branches looked like fingers from the devil that stretched towards him as if knowing that touching Marc would restore life to their limbs. The air was thick and hot, suffocating. Marc could taste the heat baking on his tongue. His mind swam in a forever buzz of alcohol.

And that hammering continued. Like steel hammering iron, its echo rang across the cemetery above Marc's head and through his ears. He didn't notice it at first, but he was gnashing his teeth. He could feel venom in his veins, infecting his mind with evil. He searched for the man in black, but all he could see were headstones and mausoleums that stretched and moaned, with shadows flitting across the graves. Marc watched the shadows. They seemed to live and breathe and moan and groan as they slithered towards him.

He stepped back, and that hammering continued, sending waves of vibration that Marc could feel echo in his bones. He could sense the man in black was here with him, as Marc watched the shadows converge, manipulated by the unseen hands of ghosts and devils. Marc watched as those shadows were summoned across his father's headstone, the gravesite rumbling beneath Marc's feet. Shadows overhead, wavering across the trees, branches, and ground towards the headstone.

And then the shift, as if the entire world moved with a loud shifting of steel that pierced Marc's ears as he cringed, gnashing his teeth. His hands were over his ears, and he clamped his eyes shut. And then… nothing.

Just the cool quiet of the wind across his skin as if he were at the edge of the universe, away from all the chaos and mayhem. Alone! He could hear and feel his heavy breathing, between his ears, inside his lungs. His innards rumbled from his core to his heart and up to his skull, as if some thick venomous energy saturated his blood, poisoning his mind, leaving an empty cavern where his heart should be.

And when he opened his eyes, the man in black was there. Tall, standing more than seven feet tall. Lanky. Dressed in black, his skin ashen with blotches of bluish green, as if his flesh were rotting with the slow precision of eternity. His black hair cascaded to his shoulders in curvy tendrils that covered his face. His dark red eyes stared incessantly at Marc. His right hand held the round, golden top of a red, wooden cane with gnarls that cascaded from the top to the bottom that looked like open mouths in the throes of a painful scream.

Marc's breath stuttered in his throat, his heart tense in his chest. And when he locked eyes with the man in black, he was greeted with a conniving grin that revealed his tiny teeth. Looked like crooked pebbles in an ocean of black. He cocked his head, as if waiting for Marc to speak.

"Pray for the devil," he said, his voice a groveled whisper that breathed into Marc's ear. "And the devil comes."

Marc had no response. He clenched his fists tight against his sides. Gritting his teeth, he glared at the man in black whose stare cut through Marc's heart.

"It's so good to see you, Marc. I've been waiting for you." He gestured to the cemetery. "Here, with the ghosts and devils of the Hollow."

A yipping holler scattered across the cemetery, echoing into the woods.

"Tell me, for what do I owe the pleasure? What catastrophe could have befallen my weary warrior to have him make the trek… all the way to me?"

"You know why I'm here. You sent your minions to find me."

The man in black grinned a tightlipped toothless grin. "Indeed," he said, then raised his chin. "This unfortunate circumstance with your beloved requires supernatural help. Assurance too, of course. Have you tried to pray? Has God not answered your desire?" And he laughed, as if to himself. Laughed and the woods howled in unison.

Marc shook his head, gritting his teeth while clenching his fists.

"Allow me to put you at ease, my dear Marc. Yes, I have the answers to your prayers, but to fulfill your request, we must work together. Only our union can restore her health."

"What is it you need me to do?"

The man in black grinned once again, his red beaming eyes glaring at Marc with pity and rage.

"Can I trust you, Marc? That is my only question. After the debacle with your mother, you cast me out, and all I wanted to do was help. Help to bring her suffering to an end. And you…"

"You manipulated me. That's not what I wanted, and you know it. I wanted her to stop the drugs, and drinking and men and…"

"Death, my good Marc, was the only way she would have stopped. She had such a weak constitution. Truly one of gods meek and weary." He clucked his tongue with a tsk, tsk, tsk, while moving his head left to right. "Think of all the suffering I spared you. Having to live with her that way. Where would such a life have taken you?"

Marc hollered, "You mesmerized me and had me cut her wrists. I was put in a psych hospital for a year. You made me look like I lost my mind…"

"Those feeble men, those doctors know nothing. Tell them the truth of what they cannot see and all they do is offer labels and diagnoses and pills by the truckload. All they do is seek to destroy what they don't understand."

Marc paused, looking away before he stepped to the man in black, his fists clenched. "We're wasting time. And I don't have a minute to spare to listen to another one of your speeches."

The man in black stiffened, standing tall, staring down at Marc. A moment later he said, "Come. Walk with me." And then, when Marc showed no signs of moving. "I must provide you with my terms and conditions. Should you agree to such, then your most prized love will greet the dawn with a renewed lease on life."

Marc studied the man in black, grinning that tightlipped smirk.

He gestured to his left. "Come," he said once again. "Walk with me."

And the man in black did just that, stepping away from the grave with his cane pressed into the desolate ground, walking further into the cemetery towards the western woods. Walking towards a mausoleum with a stone cherub on top of it. The cherub was staring at him with blood-red eyes.

The man in black called over his shoulder, "At least have enough sense to hear me out." He kept walking, his back to Marc.

"I'm sure Lori is staring down death as we speak. Seems we are a bit under the gun tonight. Perhaps you should move those legs of yours… after all, Lori doesn't have much time left."

And with that, he disappeared, and Marc's heart dropped into his stomach. The man in black reappeared, but further away, closer to the mausoleum. Marc took a step forward. Lori was waiting, and he knew she'd be healthy by morning.

The man in black will make sure of it.

41

The smell was nauseating. When a body is cut open, all those bodily fluids wreak rot into the air that lingers long after the body has been removed. Carver was standing in the office, watching forensics scrape blood off the wall with a pair of tweezers, depositing the blood in a plastic tube.

The girl, Claire, was the lucky one and Carver couldn't believe that thought ran through his mind. Claire was strangled to death, but the secretary-now identified as Lindsey Cole-was cut open while she was still alive. The sudden shock must have caused an unconscious delirium. She was still alive when Jerry removed her heart.

Ripped out her heart and then tore it into tiny bite-sized pieces that Jerry swallowed down his gullet in some mad frenzy of insanity.

What would compel Jerry to fly off the handle like this? Kill his own daughter too. Hearts? He kept talking about hearts. Hearts for the master. Carver shook his head, leaning against the credenza where Lindsey's body was found. *Who the hell is his master?*

Something wasn't adding up. Some piece to the puzzle that has yet to rear its ugly head. Carver wondered if he'd have the chance to find the missing piece. He received a call from Captain Flannery, and he wanted the day wrapped up. According to

Flannery, the murderer has been found, and Jerry Hardwood will take the fall for all three murders, including his daughter. Having lost his mind to irrational circumstances, Jerry went on a rampage. Considering his state of mind when Carver saw him, he couldn't disagree with the assumption. Nevertheless, that nagging instinct kept thumping Carver in the head.

He looked down at the chalk outline where Claire had been found. Then to the door where Jerry was hiding. He went to the door, assessing the frame, his eyes roaming over the door to the floor. Carver squatted down. There was a splatter of blood on the floor-the drippings from the bloodied heart.

Jerry seemed like a man possessed. Eating a human heart… but what would compel a man in his mid-forties to suddenly turn into a raving loon?

Carver hoped Jerry's wife would have some answers.

42

"I require a union," said the man in black. "I have been doomed to this place for longer than I care to acknowledge." He was standing in front of the mausoleum, staring eye to eye with the beaming red eyes of the cherub, with both hands wrapped around the top of his cane. Marc noticed a wooden goblet next to the cherub along with a thick and long dark green rope with a six-inch knife next to it. "I wish to be released." His voice was desperate, but Marc knew the man in black and understood how he manipulates the circumstance. Elicit emotions of empathy and compassion, then dash their hopes with ridicule and truth, then smile and embrace the subject, keeping them rattled and wondering where the truth exists.

Marc noticed how quiet the cemetery had become. Thick with quiet, as if all the creatures in hell and damnation were waiting with bated breath for the conclusion of this macabre. No more thunder, no hammering of steel against iron, no wind or lightning. All Marc could hear was the distant roar of a fire beneath the surface as if hell was cooking the earth from within.

The man in black turned slowly around, kneading his cane into the earth. He peered down at Marc, his stare unwavering. Marc could sense anger growing behind his eyes. "This is my one and only condition." The cherub looked at Marc as the man in black grinned. "Will you oblige my request?"

Marc paused before scanning across the graveyard where the shadows crept across the ground and tombstones with a sinister groan as if death was in anguish. He saw eyes staring at them from the shadows, from the darkness, in between the trees, those decayed and dying trees.

"Well, Marc? What's it going to be?" He tossed and caught his cane, pointing the golden round top at Marc. "Shall we raise Lori from the dead? Or allow her to slip into the void? Another youthful soul extinguished too soon because of tragedy." His cane drifted to the ground and the man in black leaned against it with both hands wrapped around the top. "Or allow her to die, then?" He shrugged. "Perhaps it is just her time to go? Maybe Lori Francon has had her day in the sun and death is her next adventure? The simple fact is this; Lori is going to die unless you act now. You have a choice to make, Mr. Saduj. What's it going to be?"

Marc thought about the million questions he had on his mind. He closed his eyes and breathed, the alcohol swimming in his brain, drowning all those thoughts and questions. But did they matter? What was he going to do, negotiate with Lori's life? Marc was well aware he was about to marry hell and, even more, bring hell's wrath into the fold of humanity, unleashing death upon the earth. Standing with his eyes closed, he could hear the distant beat of a dying heart. He saw Lori in his mind's eye, and he placed his hand over her heart. Her slow beating heart. Saw the light, Lori's light, beam bright from that heart. There was comfort in the light. And then, like the fragility of life and love, that light went out in a blink, and the heart that beat so slowly turned black and shriveled as if the wind carried poison.

He hoped Lori's light would find him and redeem his actions.

Marc opened his eyes, and he nodded his agreement. "Enough with the chitchat," he said. "Let the game begin."

To which the man in black laughed, cradling his cane close to his chest. "Oh Marc, you are definitely the most ambitious human *I* have ever met. A hopeless romantic if there ever was one." He paused, glaring down on Marc before he took a step back and gestured for Marc to join him by the mausoleum and the cherub in waiting. The cherub that grinned, revealing jagged black teeth accentuating his blood-red eyes. "Come. Stand and be recognized." He offered his hand and Marc cocked his head, staring at those dark, bony fingers and long nails. He looked at the man in black with his sinister grin then turned away while shaking his head. Marc gritted his teeth before he reached his hand out, taking the offered hand. The man in black pulled him closer to the mausoleum, standing Marc next to him as the cherub shifted and stood.

"Lori should thank you for your sacrifice. But worry not, all you know is about to change. The ceremony is about to begin and with it, our bond will be forever. Lori will live and breathe and all will be right in the world. You will have the knowledge that your beloved lives and I, I can finally leave this hellish limbo." And he grinned once again, his eyes gleaming in the moonlight. Marc could see fire beneath those red pupils.

And Marc wondered just how scathing hell would be.

43

Jerry's wife, Sheila, was on her second glass of wine when Carver knocked on her door. She was surrounded by family: her father and her twelve-year-old son. Carver was greeted by Sheila's father, Claude, and provided entrance to the home. The television was on mute, but he could see the local news outside of Hardwood Realty on the screen. Carver had hoped he would get to Sheila before the newscast.

Obviously, he had no such luck, just like the day's events had unfolded. Those news reporters only cared about their careers. He was surprised there wasn't a news van outside the Hardwood home already, and he hoped the story doesn't make it to the national news networks. Then he'd have a real shit show on his hands.

Claude stopped Carver in the living room. "Is it true what they're saying? That it was Jerry who did this?" His head was shaking. Carver put Claude in his mid-sixties with his gray head of hair and the way he carried himself: sophisticated and wise.

"I can't comment on an open investigation. I apologize and offer my condolences to the family."

There were tears in Claude's eyes. He wiped them off with the back of his hand. "My baby," he said. "Oh, my poor baby."

Carver put his hand on Claude's shoulder. "You've got to be there for your daughter and your grandson. They'll need you now more than ever."

Claude nodded, sucking back his tears with a sniffle.

"Where is Sheila? I have a few questions I'm hoping she can answer."

His hand over his mouth, his eyes staring lost at the floor. "She's in the bedroom. Hasn't come out since she heard what happened." He wiped his eyes again with a sniffle. "Last door down the hall."

Carver squeezed Claude's shoulder and offered his gratitude, then watched as he took his seat in the living room. He could hear Claude's choked back cries. This was the hardest part of his job, sitting with the victim's family and witnessing the heartbreak. Death was one thing, but murder was a completely different ballgame. Knowing another human being took the life of your beloved. Picturing their final moments and we all know how the mind fills in the gaps, turning those thoughts into a forever nightmare they will live with all their lives. Always second-guessing every single moment, decision, and outcome. What could I have done differently? Maybe if I wasn't so harsh when they were five, they wouldn't have been out so late, and they'd still be alive. Irrational thoughts that led to one conclusion: their loved one was never coming home and there was nothing they could do about it.

Carver turned down the hall, passing all the family pictures hanging from the wooden slats. They looked so happy in those pictures, with no sign that something sinister existed beneath the folds. The last picture before the master bedroom was of particular interest and swelled Carver's throat with a lump filled with anguish. Jerry and his daughter were at the beach. The picture must have been taken recently, maybe as recently as this past summer. Jerry had his arm around her shoulder, and they were smiling big and bright, their eyes gleaming with laughter.

Yeah, and this is the man who ripped out his daughter's heart.

The scene wasn't adding up. Not at all. He turned to the door and took a deep breath before knocking. He could hear the stuttered squelch of cries behind the door.

"Sheila? It's Detective Carver..." He paused, hoping she would answer. "I'd like to ask a few questions if that's okay?" Carver had met Sheila decades ago. He pictured her in the room, keeping quiet, maybe shaking her head or wringing her hands. He was certain she didn't want to answer his questions. Her head had to be spinning a million miles an hour.

Nothing. No sound or retort and no acknowledgement. The door on his right creaked open. Carver snapped his head to it. Standing in the door was Jerry's son, John, wearing a petrified stare. He looked lost.

"Hello," said Carver but the boy turned his eyes down, staring at the floor. He said nothing, then walked back to his bed, grabbing the stuffed lion from the floor and sat with it, stroking the lion's mane. Carver's heart sank. He rapped on the bedroom door once again. "Sheila please? I know this is difficult. I'll be as quick as possible." Nothing. Carver waited.

Maybe now wasn't the time. It's not like he was looking for the murdering pig that took Sheila's daughter. According to Captain Flannery, they had the man who committed all three murders. There was nothing pressing Carver to receive answers. Nothing pressing other than his gut instinct telling him something was off about the entire situation. He went to knock again but thought better of it. He can provide his number to Claude and request Sheila contact him to schedule appropriate questioning. Maybe it was best for him to go?

The thought dissipated the moment he heard the lock on the door click then the doorknob twisted, and the door opened a crack. He listened to footsteps padding across the room. Carver closed his eyes and took a deep breath, his hand hovering over the doorknob. He looked back at John, sitting quietly with his lion on his lap, his eyes lost in thought. The boy looked at him. His jaw hung open as if he wanted to say something, but all he did was swallow those words down his gullet and hold that lion tight against his chest before lying on his bed with his back to Carver.

He hoped someone, maybe Claude, would retrieve the boy and provide the comfort he desperately required. He was obviously lost and needed help. Carver gripped the doorknob and walked into the bedroom, shutting the door behind him. The lights were on, the room large and open, with plenty of space. Dark wood furniture occupied the room with a four-post bed, armoire, chest of drawers, and side tables beside the bed. A cloth chair sat in the corner by the windows with closed blinds and on the side table between the bed and the chair was a bottle of red wine, half empty and a wineglass next to it, half full, with lipstick marks on the rim. Sheila was sitting on the chair, blank faced, with a box of tissues on her lap on top of the blanket wrapped around her legs. She held one of those tissues, using it to blot the endless stream of tears from her eyes. She wouldn't look at him. Her head turned toward the window, her jaw resting on her fist with the tissue and her elbow on the arm of the chair.

One look and Carver wished he'd waited a day or two to question Sheila. But he needed-no, wanted-answers with the hope that she could shed some light on the current situation.

"Sheila, thank you for meeting with me. I understand how difficult this must be for you… for your family." He paused, staring at Sheila, who seemed as if she hadn't heard a word he said. "I offer my deepest sympathy and condolences." Paused again, hoping for some type of acknowledgement. "Would you like to go to the kitchen, so others are present during the interview? Or maybe allow your father to come in… so you have some support?"

Sheila closed her eyes, and Carver noticed the tears continued, streaming from beneath her eyelids. She sniffled back her tears and blotted her cheeks with the tissue before returning her stare to the window.

"I'm waiting for the news vans to arrive," she said, her voice hoarse. "I'm surprised they aren't out there already."

Good, Carver thought. At least she's not completely lost. He was hoping to gain some insight into the murders and needed Sheila coherent. He eyeballed the glass and wine bottle. Considering the half full glass and bottle, he was certain Sheila hadn't passed into an alcohol-fueled mindset. At least, not yet. She probably had just enough to help settle her nerves, if that was at all possible.

"Let's just get this over with."

Carver paused before he gestured to the bed. "May I sit?"

"Of course."

Carver took a pencil and notepad from his shirt pocket as he walked to the bed. "Just so we are clear, Sheila, I'm here professionally and not as a friend. If you'd like to have a lawyer present, we can reschedule the interview to accommodate your request."

Sheila looked at him as if he added insult to injury. More tears rolled down her cheeks.

Carver stopped cold before sitting. His heart sank with Sheila's stare.

"I have nothing to hide," she said, but Carver could feel her anger boiling beneath the surface, her voice edgy and short.

Carver sat and retrieved a recorder from his pants pocket, showing it to Sheila. "I need to record this so it's official and with the hope that this will be our one and only interview. Are you ok with it?"

Sheila eyeballed the recorder in Carver's hand before nodding her agreement.

"Thank you." Carver cleared his throat before pressing the record button, then put the recorder on the nightstand beside the wine bottle. Sheila gripped her glass and took a sip as Carver spoke, providing the date, location and person interviewed, then acknowledged himself as the interviewer. Sheila sat, ready for the interview, holding her glass-tissue tucked into her palm-with the stem on her lap.

"Mrs. Hardwood, have you noticed any change in your husband recently? Any odd behavior at all?"

To which Sheila promptly responded, "Yes. He kept complaining he was hearing whispers."

"Whispers?" Carver repeated.

"Yes, whispers. He said he heard them in the middle of the night. That he would jolt awake and thought someone was in the house and all he could hear were whispers."

Carver shook his head. "Did he mention what the whispers said?"

Sheila paused, thinking. Or perhaps she didn't want to say; perhaps she couldn't say. She pursed her lips and swallowed before taking another sip. "He said they were incoherent. Like gibberish. That they were talking so fast he couldn't understand a word they said."

Carver tightened his lips, gritting his teeth. "When did it start?"

"I'm not sure, but if I had to guess, I'd say about a week ago." Her voice trailed off with that last word, and she blotted her eyes with the tissue before taking another sip.

"Have you noticed anyone around the house, or any cars outside that were out of place, or even following you?"

Sheila shook her head and answered, "No." Then, after a pause, "Do you think someone put him up to it?"

"I'm just trying to figure out why a prominent man in the community with no history of violence… not even a previous arrest record, would suddenly fly off the handle and murder three people. It just doesn't add up."

She said nothing. No response. Her eyes drifted before she turned to the window.

Carver waited before asking his next question. "Did he say anything about some master he's following? Has he taken up any sort of new religious practices or has he been reading books on the occult or Satanism?"

Sheila looked at him through a crooked stare. Obviously, he hit a dead end.

"How about Zoe? Has she been acting strange lately? Is there anything you can think of that has been out of the ordinary?"

Sheila just shook her head. "There's nothing Stephen. Nothing except for the whispers. But I just thought it was stress."

Carver's instincts perked up. "Stress?"

Sheila nodded. "Jerry has been under a great deal of stress lately, especially since his father passed. He said the business wasn't doing as well as he had thought it was. Apparently, his father had a property that he refused to sell that was eating into the company's profits. Jerry planned on selling it as soon as possible."

"What property?"

Sheila turned to the window, as if she could see through the blinds. "It's an old house in the western woods, surrounded by acres of land. It's worth millions to the right developer."

Carver turned his attention to the window. He knew the western woods were outside beyond the Hardwood home. Legend has it the woods were haunted, and Carver felt his blood turn cold.

"I wasn't aware there were any houses in the woods. How old is it?"

"Centuries according to Jerry. But the house has been vacant for a long time. He planned on bulldozing the structure but figured whoever bought it would do the same, so he kept it up to spare the cost of destruction." She finished her drink, then placed the glass on the table.

Carver paused before he changed direction, inquiring about Jerry's relationships with Lindsey, Claire, and, of course, his daughter, Zoe. All questions that received viable and unremarkable answers with no detail pertaining to why Jerry flew off the handle. He was as confused now as he was before he knocked on the door. He also noticed that with every question, Sheila seemed to turn more inward, lost and hollow.

He offered his condolences again and thanked her for the interview. Sheila did not respond, her eyes downcast. He waited, but when it was obvious that she had retreated into the dark recesses of fear and heartache, Carver opened the door. His plan was to inform Sheila's father about her condition and to advise him to keep a watchful eye on her.

But the moment he opened the door, Sheila whispered, "Initium Novum."

Carver turned around. He knew the Latin phrase was kept out of the public eye. "Where did you hear that?"

Sheila looked like she'd just been punched in the gut, her body tense and her eyes wide as if she were responding to internal stimuli.

"Sheila?" No response. "Where did you hear that from?"

Sheila turned to him. "Humanity's end as a new beginning."

"Yes," said Carver, "But where did you hear it?"

"The whispers."

"Are you hearing them now?"

Sheila nodded, looking around the room. "They're here now. In the room. Can you hear them?"

Carver looked around. "No, Sheila, I don't hear anything." He paused as he cleared his throat. "What are they saying?" Quite obvious to Carver that Sheila was entering a phase towards insanity. He only hoped it would not lead down the same path as Jerry. He needed to bring in a mental health professional. A call he will make in a moment. "Sheila?" She looked at him and a sudden darkness fell over her eyes. "What are they saying?"

"Humanity's end as a new beginning," she repeated, and stood up. "I can see it. They're showing me what will happen." The blanket fell to the floor and Carver couldn't help but notice the revolver in her hand. She must have had it under the blanket.

"Sheila, please. Put the gun down. Your son, your only son, is in the next room."

She looked like she was battling an internal thought. "I have to. It's the only way he'll gain the strength to stop them."

"Who are you talking about?"

Her body stiffened. Her teeth chattered. "My son," she said and shot herself in the head.

44

The cherub cut the dark green rope in the center. The rope had been wrapped around Marc's right wrist, tied into a knot, and the remaining thread wrapped around the wrist of the man in black's left hand, tied into a knot again, and pulled tight. According to the man in black, they were now bound together with a single purpose: to allow Lori to live.

Marc had been in a trance during the ceremony. With tears in his eyes, he listened to the cherub speaking in Latin with words and declarations Marc did not understand. The cherub used the blade to cut Marc's wrist, just a small cut, but it bled into the goblet. He did the same to the man in black. Marc tasted the salty fluid on his lips as he drank from the goblet then watched while the man in black did the same. His lips curled into a grin when the blood graced his tongue, racing down his throat.

Marc noticed those eyes in the darkness grew wide when the cherub cut the string. He heard the held breath from the dead gasp across the cemetery as if they relished the moment. All else was quiet, but Marc could feel the fire rising beneath the earth as if Satan himself was climbing out of the bog of internal earth. His scar burned across his skull. He pressed against it, releasing blood that cascaded across his brow and down across his nose.

"My lord," said the man in black. "You're bleeding."

The sting from the wound was irritating, driving Marc into a frenzy. He used his sleeve to blot the blood from his watery, burning eye and nose. "Is it done?" asked Marc, looking at the blood on his sleeve and avoiding the stare he knew was burrowing into his soul. When he received no answer, he turned to the man in black. "You got what you wanted. Now bring Lori back."

And the man in black grinned, glaring at Marc, devouring him with his eyes. "As you wish." He lifted his cane and turned around, dipping the cane as if to some invisible wall. Marc looked up as energetic ripples bubbled across the sky. He could see Lori inside those blips of light, sitting on a hospital bed, awake and healthy.

Marc stepped closer. Lori's image was projected over fifty feet across the dark sky. Her lips called for him. "Where is Marc?" she said, her head craned as if searching for him when the image paused. Marc smiled, smiled for the first time since he left the cabin.

"Can't believe it," he whispered, his eyes fixed on Lori. "You actually did it. For the first time, you came through on your promise. You…" He turned, but the man in black was no longer there. Nothing but the cold and dark cemetery greeted him. Even the cherub had returned to its stone state, sitting on the mausoleum as if standing in protection of the dead when the image of Lori faded into the night sky. Marc stepped further into the cemetery, searching behind mausoleums and headstones and trees and hills. His heart jumping in his chest.

Beneath the surface, he could hear a low rumbling, a groan and a moan, as if all the dead were suddenly awakened. Heard whispers behind his ear and felt hot breath across the nape of his neck.

"We are one now, Marc Saduj. You and I bonded in holy matrimony." The man in black's voice was like a whisper in his ear.

Marc's skin crawled as goosebumps dashed across his arms. He paused while listening to the whispers but couldn't shake the feeling of pending doom writhing in his bones. He looked up, scanning across the tombstones to the rock wall surrounding the graveyard. He hurried to it.

"Spend some time, Mr. Saduj. The western woods have waited for you for decades. Meet some new friends. They deserve respite."

The rock wall was coming closer. Panic struck his heart and lungs.

"I will take up the mantle and put right what once went wrong."

He could hear laughter in his ear.

"We are one now. And in this time, only one shall prevail."

Marc vaulted over the rock wall, and when he landed, he was still in the cemetery, staring at the cherub and listening to the ear-piercing groan from the dead.

"You'll have your time again. But for now, stay awhile. Get reacquainted with some old friends. I have work of my own to tend to. There's so much to do. We must prepare for the coming of wrath and damnation."

Marc scanned across the cemetery as the dead rose in ghostly visions of anguish and hate.

45

Carver was finishing his conversation with a paramedic when Captain Flannery gestured for him to join him. The street outside the Hardwood residence was packed with squad cars, ambulances, and neighbors. There was a news van on site too. The reporter was interviewing neighbors.

Carver provided a thank you to the paramedic and then walked over to Flannery.

"Well, this is a grade A shit show," Flannery said, looking over Carver's shoulder to the swarm outside the Hardwood residence.

Carver followed his gaze. "Yeah, something like that." He turned back to Flannery.

"What the hell happened in there, detective?"

"Suicide," he said with a cracked voice. When Flannery kept silent, Carver continued. "I was questioning Sheila about the murders, hoping to shed some light on the motive and what would compel Jerry to fly off the handle. When I was done, she stood up and shot herself…"

"You didn't notice she was holding a gun?"

Carver shook his head. "She had it under a blanket on her lap. I never would have suspected…"

"After all that's happened today, you should have waited to question her. Now I've got an even bigger shit show on my hands." He gestured to the reporter and news van. "Fuckin leeches are getting fat on fresh blood and all in my city. Commissioner's gonna have my ass by tomorrow and what am I going to tell him?"

"Start with the truth. Jerry Hardwood lost his mind and killed three people, including his daughter and his wife couldn't stand the pressure and thought it was better to swallow a bullet than face the future."

"Yeah, shot herself while being questioned in her home in her bedroom of all places. This whole situation stinks to high heaven."

"I'm sorry, Captain."

"Yeah, I'm sorry too." He paused then, and Carver felt it coming. "You're on leave, one month with pay while the investigation concludes. I just got off the phone with IA. They'll be contacting you soon for a full interview."

Carver shook his head. "Can't do it, sir. There's more to this story than we know. I can't give up and give in."

"Well, you don't have a choice now, do you? Situations over, Carver. Jerry Hardwood flew off the handle and went on a murdering rampage, and that's all anyone needs to know. The why behind it is just fodder for the news. Some other detective will piece it together."

Carver gritted his teeth, turning away from Flannery and shaking his head. Scanning the chaos and mayhem, he saw the boy,

John, with his head in the window, staring lost into the void of despair. Staring at him.

My son. Bang!

Carver twitched with the remembrance of the gunshot and the sound that echoed across the sky, shaking the walls in the master bedroom. Her brain had splattered across the blinds before she fell back, cracking the window with the back of her head then dropped to the floor with a thud. Carver had stood in the bedroom, in shock, with his jaw on the floor. He could hear the gunshot like a distant roar echoing across the sky.

"You're in shock, detective. I should have taken you off the case the moment I heard Hardwood was involved. I know he's been an acquaintance of yours. For that I apologize, but it is what it is. As I said, one month with pay and make sure you attend IA's inquiries. I expect your report on my desk in the morning. At that time, consider yourself officially on leave."

Carver couldn't take his eyes off the boy. His sister and mother were dead, and his father was going to prison for the rest of his days. Carver was certain that when the boy woke up this morning, his wildest dreams and most vivid imagination could not have predicted the events that have unfolded today.

"Detective!" Flannery raised his voice, and Carver turned to him. "Did you hear me?"

"Yes, loud and clear. Report on your desk in the morning, then take leave."

"And be sure to attend IA's inquiry. I want to put this matter behind us as soon as possible. Clear?"

"Crystal clear."

"And stay away from the reporters. I don't need them twisting your words before IA has it out with you."

Carver nodded. "You have nothing to worry about there, Captain." Carver despised reporters.

Flannery took a good look at him, assessing. "This is over, detective. Make sure it stays that way."

"Understood."

Flannery held out for another moment. "Now go, detective. It's better that you're no longer here." And with that he walked away, to the house where he met with a few uniformed officers and instructed them to follow him inside.

Carver watched him enter the home, obviously on his way to question Sheila's father. He shifted his gaze to the window and the boy with the sad and lost stare.

It's the only way he can stop their tirade.

What the hell was she talking about?

He looked over to the western woods standing in the darkness as if waiting to devour life and circumstance. As if waiting to be fed fresh souls. He could feel how his breath turned shallow, constricted, as if staring into the woods stole the air from his lungs. He turned back to the window, but the boy was no longer there, the blinds waving in the window. Gone!

And what Carver knew most at that moment was that this was all far from over. Despite what Flannery thought.

46

Wren could feel his master's presence, the energy thickening the closer he came to the house. As if he brought all the fear and death from the western woods with him like an energetic chemtrail writhing off his shoulders, connecting him to the western woods.

The house shook as if awakening from its century-long slumber, welcoming the master to its dark embrace. Wren waited in the living room, standing away from the front doors as the floorboards started lifting one at a time with a red beaming glow beneath them, as if death were begging to be released. Wren looked at the bottle of Absinthe cradled in his arms, where a red glow beamed bright in the bottle's bottom.

"Our time is now," whispered Wren. "The master has come."

The doors burst open with a rush of wind and standing in the entrance was Wren's master. A cane in his right hand, red wood and thick. The master's hands were long and bony. His hair, a carpeted fuzz and Wren couldn't help but notice the scar beneath his hair, stitched to just above his left eye. He was tall and thin and smelled of death and rot. One eye burning red, the other a frosted blue. His teeth were all sharp and pointed, as if his jaw was constructed to tear flesh off the bone. Wren understood that the master was manifesting his true form through the new host's body, the same as he's done before. In time his true form will be complete.

Wren dropped to his knees, placing the bottle next to him as he bowed and kowtowed, his forehead on the boards that continued to quake in the master's presence. "My master," Wren groaned. "I honor thee." He raised his head, gazing at his master who stepped across the threshold, his cane tapping the floor. When the master moved it was as if his shadow followed a second after, as if there were a thousand masters-carbon copies that raced to catch up to the host body. He stopped in front of Wren, who wrapped his arms around the master's waist.

"It is I who honors you," said the master, returning Wren's embrace. "Your loyalty has made this all possible."

"I live to serve your will, my master."

"Rise, my friend. We have much to do before life's breath begins to force itself from my lungs."

Wren took the bottle off the floor as he rose. "The transformation liquid." Wren held the bottle for the master, who graced the bottle with his fingertips.

"Perfect." The master bit into his wrist, snapping his teeth into a vein. His lips and teeth stained with blood, he stretched his bleeding wrist to the bottle as Wren squeezed the cork from the bottleneck. A sweet fragrance followed, one comprising alcohol and candy. Wren held the open bottleneck to the master's wrist, and watched as blood rolled into the bottle, mixing with the green glowing liquid within when Wren noticed the green rope tied around the master's wrist. "When I am weak with life, I must return to the ether, to rest and gather strength. It is then that the host will return to the body. Once my strength is replenished, provide the drink to the host and I will return to this body."

"As you wish." Wren squeezed the cork into the bottleneck as the master touched the bottle with his fingertips.

"Keep it hidden, Wren. Someplace safe. Once the bottle is finished my transformation will manifest exponentially, brought to fruition with the aid of vibration and completed with the desecration of the heart."

Wren bowed to the master. "Of course. And what has befallen our weary warrior? The host in our macabre?"

The master grinned before he answered. "He waits with the ghosts in the western woods, guarded by the dead in Sleepy Hollow Cemetery. Waiting for his return to this mortal coil, and upon each return, more confusion, and even more despair. Until the day when the dead are his only refuge, and he seeks to never return to earthly form."

"And what of the girl? When will she return?"

"In time, my friend. In time. We have much to do to prepare for her arrival. All must be set by then; all must be in place to greet her appropriately. She is the last key to my complete transformation."

"Whatever needs to be done, I am willing to do. I follow your lead. Bring me into the fold of Xibalba with all the power of death and hate."

The master touched Wren's chin, his lips tight and hooked in a grin. He then looked around the house. "A bit drab, don't you think? How a century of neglect can cause such decay." He turned to Wren. "We will breathe new life into our abode. The house wants to eat. We shall provide it with what it needs."

"The basement waits for you, but the power has faded." Wren bowed, looking down, away from his master's gaze. "I am ashamed of my failure to conjure Xibalba." He returned his stare to the master. "Perhaps your power can unleash it?"

The master raised his cane to eye level. "Perhaps it requires a greater strength than both of us. After waiting so long in the ether, my power has weakened with time. We must open the portal. My ghost demons are waiting. They wait to be unleashed on the earth and to bathe humanity in darkness." He looked up to the ceiling as if he could see beyond the roof. "I can hear them calling from across the universe. They have assembled their army and are preparing for our victory."

"The universe conspires for our success. The time has come for the darkness to be unleashed on the light. To turn love into hate and God into an afterthought. In the future, the universe belongs to darkness."

"Indeed," said the master. "Now, shall we see what state of decay has become of our dungeon? Allow me to know how far we must reach to awaken the portal and how much blood must be sacrificed to unleash its full power."

"As you wish, my master." Wren bowed. "As you wish."

47

In the dream, Lori could see death as if it lived and breathed in the red eyes of the man in black. She was running lost in the woods and every moment when she believed she was about to leap from the bounds of the woods she returned to where she started. As if life were a continuous struggle that looped back to the same catastrophe.

She could never find her way out. Could never locate the heart of the matter, the one that would allow her to leave the woods. No matter how far she ran or how loud she screamed, she could never break free from the chains of those woods. Listening to the distant sound of thunder rumbling above the earth like an impending doom that thickened in her chest, poisoning every atom in her body.

Over time, she concluded the woods had become her eternal home, and the moment she accepted this dire fate was the moment the dream slipped into the void. Behind it, she could hear the slow bleep, bleep, bleep of her heart. A sound that was accompanied by the overpowering scent of rubbing alcohol and rotting death. As if all the dead people in the woods emitted a nasty, decaying breath all at once. And with that sound and that stench, Lori opened her eyes. The dream dissipated, filtering from consciousness into the dark recesses of the subconscious, tucked away and best forgotten.

Lori's eyes hurt when she opened them, as if the overhead light sought to squeeze anguish into her brain. The vitals monitor bleeped along with her heart. The room spiraled into focus. White, clean, and bright with light. She could see the nurse's station outside her room where two nurses engaged in small talk she could not hear. Her stomach squeezed her innards as if all her organs were suddenly awakened and restarted the long labor to keep life in the fold of the body, aching after a long slumber.

Her eyelids fluttered, her eyes adjusting to the light. Elena was sleeping on a cot in the corner. Lori's breathing was shallow, her breath thick in her lungs as she attempted to remember. To understand where she was and what was happening. Struggling to conjure a memory from the void of her mind.

What happened? Marc?

Thoughts she couldn't latch on to. Thoughts that dissipated from consciousness at the same moment they entered as if they sought to avoid her understanding. So many thoughts spiraled through her brain, but she couldn't find the first thought. The one that would tell her what had happened. She felt dense, as if her brain refused to work, struggling to find a memory.

"Oh my. Thank goodness."

Lori's head throbbed. She reached her hand to her forehead, feeling the bandage wrapped tight around her head. Her eyes drifted to the nurse standing over her.

"I can't believe it," the nurse said, staring, assessing, studying Lori's eyes. "The doctor tried one last surgery. I can't believe it worked. It's a miracle." She was talking as if Lori wasn't there. Lori noticed her mother twitched across the cot. The nurse smiled. "It's good to have you back. We were quite concerned."

Lori went to speak, but her throat hurt as if she'd swallowed razor blades and her mouth was dry like desert heat.

"It's okay, save your strength," said the nurse while examining the vitals monitor.

Lori managed to squeeze one word over her lips. "Marc?" she asked, receiving a skeptical stare from the nurse. "Where is Marc?"

To which the nurse cocked her head and said, "Who?"

"Can you feel the energy, Wren?" asked the man in black. They were in the basement. Wren stood in front of the pedestal with the crystal bowl on top that was drenched in Zoe Hardwood's blood. He was watching his master standing in front of the three openings, assessing, his cane in his right hand, his left arm draped across his navel, palm up. He looked up to the ceiling, and Wren followed his gaze. "It's magnificent, isn't it?"

"Indeed. The energy is pulsing across every atom. It calls to us all the way from Xibalba. Begging to be unleashed upon humanity."

The room beyond those three openings was bathed in darkness, as if the darkness guarded what the room held in its embrace. Wren couldn't see more than a few inches into the darkness before the pitch-blackness refused the eye to follow any further.

"Has the energy gone sour?" asked Wren. "Stale. Perhaps resulting from the lack of sacrifice?"

The man in black turned to Wren, his head cocked to the right. Wren marveled over his master's transformation. The host's body blended the master's ethereal features with the solid substance of the host's flesh and bone, the union's blood pulsing through the body's veins. "The witch who condemned me to the ether put a hex on my chamber," said the man in black. "You made the necessary sacrifice to reverse the spell?" His eyes narrowed, and Wren noticed he gripped his cane tight.

"I have, with the heart born from the lineage of your persecutors, as you instructed," said Wren with a bow. "But with no recourse to a solution. The witch completed her duty with success. I am at a loss on what to do."

The man in black raised his cane. "Let us see if the magic born from the cane can unlock the witch's spell. Entering my chamber is only the first hurtle to overcome." He turned to the openings. "I am confident in the cane's ability, but it is the portal to Xibalba existing beyond these walls that will require time, patience… and sacrifice." He stepped closer to the openings, raising his cane to eye level then twisted the golden round top when a green-grayish smoke slithered from the cane. "With all of damnation and wrath, I command you to allow me entrance." The man in black talked to the smoke and Wren could see the glimmer of eyes within that green-grayish smoke, with mouths revealing jagged teeth that snapped as if capturing prey within its jaws.

The smoke slithered across the openings, charging the darkness that crackled like an electrical outlet, pulsing energy from its mouth. The smoke recoiled like a snake, hissing across the openings, then darted into the folds of darkness. The man in black raised his arms, tense and constricted as if he were squeezing with all his strength.

"Come to me, my humble abode. It has been too long. I seek refuge within your dark embrace."

Wren watched wide-eyed as the entrances glowed with a faint red and orange radiance, growing bright and then wavering, then bright again.

The man in black, holding the cane, squeezed his arms as if he were embracing an apparition, his arms tense and shuddering as his hands came together, gripping his cane tight as he roared and smoke barreled from the cane with the force of a hurricane that raced across the entrances, battling the witch's energetic spell. The smoke consumed the spell, swallowing the electric field as that red-orange glow brightened.

And then an explosion, rippling an energetic burst across the man in black when Wren was tossed backward, dropping onto his back then sliding to the wall behind him with a thud. His master remained standing, with his arms outstretched as if he embraced the explosion.

He did it. The master opened the chamber, reversing the witch's spell. Wren gathered himself to his feet, staring at the entrances that were still bathed in black, although something had changed. Wren could feel it, like a release of energy, knowing the witch's spell was no more.

His master had shared stories about the torture chamber he was about to enter. The blood that was spilled in that room could fill all the oceans on the earth. He could hear the cries from the dead;

the painful blood-curdling screams existed like an energetic stain in the chamber.

Wren stepped forward, taking the crystal bowl from the floor and raising the pedestal that had been tossed to the ground from the explosion. His eyes were on his master, standing motionless, staring into the darkness that coated the entrances. His master gripped his cane tight and stepped closer to the opening, stopping just outside, craning his head, staring, assessing, before he dipped his head in then stepped in and vanished. Wren noticed a wave of energy cascaded across the entrance when he entered. Wren gazed at the openings, amazed that all he could see was blackness.

"Come, Wren," said the master. "There is no reason to be afraid."

Wren stepped into the darkness as an electrical pulse rippled through his body and the heat ramped into overdrive. Like stepping into a new world or a different dimension.

The room was circular, vast, and made from stone. It occupied the entire expanse of the house above. From where Wren stood at the entrances from the basement the dungeon stretched a hundred feet away from him and over two hundred feet to either side. Sconces were lined up across the walls and were all lit by the master's magic, bathing the dungeon in a red-orange glow. Wren was certain they were below the third-floor room of the house. He looked up and grinned. The ceiling was high; he had to stretch his neck back to see all of it.

There was a cage hanging from the ceiling over his shoulder, above the entrances to the basement, and a pendulum hanging from the rafters high above. The pendulum hovered above the waist-high rock slab that was shaped like a cross in the center of the room with leather straps on all sides of the cross. A large and round, waist high firepit stood beside the slab, coated with dust. Hanging from the walls were a host of wrist and ankle shackles, secured to the walls. Enough to imprison a host of sacrifices in waiting.

Across the room on his left were all the torture devices the master had promised, all in various states of decay and neglect. Wren couldn't help the small smile that curled in the corner of his mouth while he dreamed of the torture he'll be doling out soon. He then gazed over the rock slab and what he believed was a coat of dried blood, turned brown with age stained into the rock, on the stone floor and smeared across the walls. A small alcove on his far right reached into darkness. Wren noticed a foul stench, like sewage and rot, coming from that alcove.

On the other end of the chamber, across from where he stood, was a mirror image of the entrances they walked through from the basement. They were the same size and mold, but with one major difference. Three tall wooden doors with pointed tops were embedded in the wall. It was here that his master had gone, assessing the thick wooden doors that seemed out of place to Wren. As if they weren't doors but were meant as a deterrent to anyone who wished to enter. The master placed his hand on the wood.

"Is it the portal?" asked Wren. "The cave where you first tasted human flesh. Our method to commune with the devils of Xibalba?" And when he didn't answer, his master's head bowed with his forehead to the door, Wren asked, "How can we open them?"

The man in black turned to Wren, his cane kneading into the stone floor. He looked down at his body. "When I am whole, and only when I am whole, will I have the strength to unleash the full force of Xibalba. And that right will come in time, after the arrival of our star-crossed lover." He turned back to the entrances. "The portal carries its own existence. It travels into the ether through the astral plane to Xibalba. Much the same as the mausoleum where my ghost demons wait. But the portal holds more capabilities than the cemetery, allowing the essence of evil to slither into this world. The cemetery was built on sacred ground." He shook his head then clucked his tongue. His head down as if in silent contemplation. "It offers a way one ticket and nothing else." He looked over his shoulder. "But the strength of the astral plane in the portal is different." He looked up, his voice a whisper. "A form of hell in and of itself to those who know no better. Where evil and our most dire fears exist." He turned to Wren. "We must strengthen the astral portal while we wait for my full transformation. Charge it and power it so that charge reaches into Xibalba, and I can whisper to my people to prepare for our time on earth."

Wren ran his tongue across his lips, staring at the doors. "How do we strengthen the energy in the portal? What must be done?"

To which his master responded, "Sacrifice, my dear Wren. Sacrifice!"

49

Lori watched as the nurse returned to her station. She had to admit, she felt absolutely capital, as if her long coma brought with it a renewed thirst for life. Felt like she was beaming bright with energy, peaceful in her heart, as if she were dipped in magical waters. Her thoughts were clear, poised, and sharp. The nurse expected her to be in pain, but no pain had arrived since she'd awakened. Her wounds had healed overnight. It was a miracle, indeed.

The nurse said the doctor would be in to see her soon. She'll be transferred to a private room on another floor in the hospital to run some more tests. The doctors wanted to be certain there were no additional ailments that had yet to surface, but by all indications Lori seemed perfectly healthy. Although, with her mother's presence, she knew something had happened between Elena and Marc. She wanted him here, wanted her mother gone and Marc by her side. And when the nurse was out of earshot, she addressed her mother.

"Where is he? Where is Marc?" She shook her head. "You shouldn't be here. He should be." Her jaw was tight, her eyes like daggers.

Elena pursed her lips and cleared her throat, sitting next to Lori by her bedside. She cupped her hands, and Lori could see she was stalling. She wanted to rip her mother's head off, despising the silence and her mother's blatant stalling.

"Tell me *now!*" She shouted that last word, and the air thickened with tension.

Elena glared at Lori, disapprovingly. Lori had seen that stare all her life. The one that said she was not pleased with the current situation, but even more, she was not pleased with Lori's outburst. "Why am I always to blame? I've sat by your bed since the day you arrived. You think it's fun sleeping on a cot the way I have?" She shook her head and turned away, her jaw resting in her hand.

Another Elena tactic, gaslighting was one of the woman's go-to methods for deterrence. Lori wasn't having it.

"Stop gaslighting, this is not on me. He had to have come here. I know Marc better than he knows himself. There's no way he wouldn't have come to see me."

Elena turned her stare to Lori. Her jaw tight, her eyes like two dark pins, staring wretchedly at her own daughter. "I'd rather not have to tell you this right now, considering your current situation and the fact that you should rest and recuperate...."

Lori shook her head. "Enough with the speech. Can you just get on with it? And I want the truth, not your version of events, which you so delicately twist in your favor."

Elena grinded her teeth; her nose crinkled in a sneer.

"Mom, tell me the truth."

"The truth?"

"Yes, the truth."

"Very well, let's have the truth. Yes, he came here, of course he did, little rat that he is. He took one look at you and he couldn't handle the situation. He left Lori. Left you here to rot and die on your own."

Again, Lori was shaking her head. "That's a lie. I know Marc wouldn't leave my side unless he was forced to." She pointed at her mother. "And you must have done something to force him out." Her hands were shaking, teeth grinding. She could beat her mother with a stick right now if she had one.

"Well, aren't you ungrateful?" She pushed herself out of the chair, then walked to the opposite side of the room to the black duffle bag on the floor in the corner.

"What are you doing?" asked Lori, her voice dropped, concerned over her mother's actions.

Elena unzipped the side pocket on the duffle bag and retrieved a small white envelope.

"What is that?"

Elena shook her head as she walked back to the bed. "Well, don't take my word for it, since I'm a liar and all." She offered Lori the envelope. "He wrote you a letter."

Lori stared at the envelope, crinkled in her mother's palm. She laughed and huffed. "Please, mother, I'm sure you wrote that letter yourself." She turned away, afraid she would not be receiving the truth, or any part of it, for that matter. Not with her mother here.

"Again, with the mistrust." Elena placed the envelope on Lori's lap. "You can read it for yourself. You'll see it's his handwriting." Lori turned to her mother, now walking around the bed. "I'm famished, and I need food. I'm going to the cafeteria. Do you want something?"

Lori shook her head, glaring at Elena when she gestured to the envelope.

"I'll let you read that on your own. As I said, you'll recognize his handwriting. I'm sure you're aware of his unique scribble but if you're still under the impression that I could pull off such a ruse ask the nurse, Jessica, when she arrives and she'll confirm that Marc…" she pointed to the envelope, "-wrote that letter. She's the one who gave him the paper and envelope. And then maybe you'll apologize for your accusations." She locked eyes with Lori. "Or not." She shrugged. "But I'm done with this conversation and with all things Marc Saduj."

She turned on her heels and left. Lori watched as she walked through the ICU entrance then turned to the letter sitting on her lap. She wanted nothing to do with it. Yes, Marc had unique handwriting, like something out of an old-world horror novel, a mix of cursive and print that to any novice would seem as if two completely different people penned the same letter. Yes, it would be difficult, very difficult indeed, for someone to forge Marc's handwriting.

Lori pursed her lips and cleared her throat, fighting every impulse that warned her not to open that envelope. She tore the top, pulled out the letter and unfolded the paper. Her eyes widened when she saw the handwriting.

Without a doubt, the letter was written by Marc.

And the content sunk Lori's heart into the depths of despair.

50

Wren followed his master into the dark corner of the dungeon to the alcove where the horrid stench was coming from. He was surprised when he found stone steps-six of them-in the alcove that led down beneath the house to a landing that twisted around to three more stone steps that emptied into a wide and dark opening. The ground was earth, dirt and stones and the smell was rancid with sewage. Wren crinkled his nose to ward off the rot from invading his nostrils, but with no such luck. The putrid, vile stench was everywhere. The room was cold. Wren felt a chill nip into his bones even through his overcoat.

"What is this?" asked Wren, his voice echoing in the darkness. He stepped into a puddle of sludge, and his boots came away with a wet squish. The stench drifted to his nostrils, and he immediately turned away. He recognized the stench. The smell reminded him of methane. Wren investigated the large area in front of him. There were four passages, each leading in different directions. He turned to address his master.

The man in black was admiring the room, completely comfortable with the smell. The darkness seemed to wrap itself around him as if embracing an old friend. The room was so dark Wren could barely see his hand in front of him, let alone his master standing close to him. If it weren't for the red cane faded into the blackness and the whites from his eyes beaming bright like floodlights, he wouldn't have known he was there.

"The revolution," said the master. "We are standing on old ground. The patriots at the time required access to the Hudson. Access that allowed them to slip past the enemy without being seen with a method to bring supplies to their weary battalions." He pointed to the halls with his cane. "It was the construction of these tunnels that reawakened the cave so many years ago, offering me the ability to whisper into the ear of our predecessor to build the house. It represents the very center of the western woods where the portal, the cave in this world had formed, and these passages played perfectly into our plan. They reach the four corners of Sleepy Hollow. To the Hudson further west, and the cemetery in the north. Further east and south too, which, when they were first constructed, allowed for the rise of battalions from West Point during the revolution. Now these tunnels are ours to do with as we please. They meet our needs perfectly."

Wren followed his master's gaze.

"We can come and go through Sleepy Hollow as we wish, unseen by prying eyes. These tunnels have been forgotten by those above ground. They are ours to use as we desire."

"Remarkable," said Wren, his voice a hush that echoed through the halls.

"When our host has resurfaced, at no time is he allowed downstairs." The master looked up and around. "At no time is he allowed to discover the dungeon. Not until I give the order. He must be kept in the dark over our dealings down here until the time is right. Do you understand, Wren?"

Wren bowed to his master. "Of course. Whatever you will me to do, I choose to serve."

"Thank you, Wren." And he turned around, leaning on his cane. "Enough with the tour. There is work for us to do. So much to do, Wren. Winter is coming and with it, the stars will be aligned to capture my full transformation and open the portal. Until then, we must prepare for the coming of a new dawn where all of humanity will bow to our whim. Now, come Wren." He stepped to the six stone steps. "I feel our host has been introduced to some old friends. My bones grow heavy with his fear. Before they tear his mind apart, there are things that need to be in place before he returns to the host body."

He shuffled dutifully to the steps. Wren looked around the room, his nose crinkled from the stench of methane.

"What a putrid and foul place this is." He turned to the steps, seeing that red cane move inside the dark. He closed his eyes, shaking his head to ward off the poisonous stench. His master was gone now, up the steps, and Wren followed, as he was told.

51

He heard the creak of bones and the groan from the dead before he saw them. Shadows in the cemetery, clawing at headstones.

Marc knew he was not alone.

You little shit. What did you do?

He could hear his mother's voice, on repeat, echoing across the cemetery. His heart was jumping in his chest, pounding in his ears with a thunderous boom as he ran further into the cemetery, attempting to get away. To evade the old-time fears wishing for revenge.

Look what you did to me!

He stopped abruptly, his feet skidding across wet earth and grass. His bones felt heavy, weighted down as if the bones had grown dense. It was difficult to keep up, to keep running. He gasped for breath and bent over, hands on his knees. His skin was pulsing with heat, but the air was cool, battling with his internal temperature. Felt a hand press against the nape of his neck and he jumped and turned, listening to the cackling laugh that echoed across the cemetery.

Then, as if the same mouth that laugh had come from was suddenly cut off, *Look what you did to me!*

"I didn't do anything," he hollered. "It was the man in black. You know I wouldn't hurt you."

Saw his mother standing in the distance, behind a headstone. An apparition, flickering under the light of the moon. Her finger in her mouth, and he could see blood across her wrists, cascading down her arm where it pooled in the crux of her elbow and dripped to the ground as she laughed and cackled. He stepped forward, staring at his mother.

"I'm so sorry."

He watched as she flickered and vanished, and all in the cemetery grew quiet and still. He tried to remember, to remember where he came from and how he came to be in the cemetery. Why did he have so much trouble leaving? It seemed that every turn led to the same mausoleum, the same cherub standing guard and waiting. As if he were running in an endless loop to the same destination, his frustration squeezing the memory from conscious thought. Never able to find the missing link.

The snap of a twig on his right and Marc's heart jumped then skipped a few beats. He took off running again, then found himself staring eye to eye with the cherub. A certain whine escaped his throat. Trapped. A living prisoner among the dead and tortured. And he could feel it, the presence in the cemetery looking to devour his fear and eat it raw. He could feel its energy creeping towards him like an abyss of darkness. A void Marc knew he should not enter. Felt it racing towards him and Marc turned to the cherub. Now he could hear the fear as if it had grown legs and was barreling towards him. It groaned and moaned over his shoulder, creeping towards him, breathing down his neck. He kicked the door to the mausoleum, frantic and hurried. Noticed his scar itched like a madman, hell-bent on revenge. Pulsing and throbbing with an infection tainting his blood. Tainting his mind. He kicked and then pushed, slamming his shoulder into the door, sensing the fear and darkness inching closer to him.

"Please," he whined, then stepped back and rushed at the door that buckled under his weight and tore open. And Marc fell. Fell into the mouth of darkness. The cemetery was now gone, and all he could see was darkness. His breath was heavy and labored. Sweat on his forehead-or was it blood-wet and slick. He pushed on his scar and pain rattled across his skull. His eyeball was swollen, burning, tearful and throbbing.

He looked around, frantic, his eyes darting from left to right and all around but all he could see was black, like ink that swallowed him whole. There were no edges to the mausoleum. No beginning and no end. Just pitch black, with depths as large as the universe. Marc stepped back, stepped back and away, hearing the hum begin. It started low, but Marc understood the hum was only beginning. Now a blue hue, like the blue from a fire, lifted off the ground. And then a loud boom, like a giant stomping. On his right. On his left. Behind him. He whipped around.

Saw teeth snapping its jaws towards his face and Marc screamed. Devoured by the darkness.

52

Carver couldn't get the boy's stare out of his head. Sitting at his desk, staring at the report with a pencil in his hand, he had yet to write one word. He noticed his hand was shaking.

My son. Bang!

He heard Sheila's voice and the hard boom from the gun. Then the bullet ripped through her head and then the boy, John, was staring at him through the window. Lost. What tragedy had that boy endured today? His sister had her heart ripped out. His father, the murdering heart eating son of a bitch who did it. Also killing two more people. Then his mother put a bullet in her head in some hopped up insanity to save him. What could he say in his report to tie it all together? The truth and that was it. The truth according to the bend of reality.

But what Carver knew all too well was that there was something that wasn't adding up. Some elusive piece of information that would tie this all together. He knew Jerry Hardwood, and the man wasn't someone who just went off the handle like that. There had to be something driving him to commit a triple homicide. But he saw him, Carver did. Saw how insane Jerry was acting.

Hearts for the master?

Initium Novum.

Humanity's end as a new beginning.

What the fuck is going on?

As a police officer, a detective no less, the answer was always simple and the guy holding the knife was always the killer. Jerry had definitely murdered Lindsey and Claire, although his daughter was another story. But with all the evidence against him, it was difficult for Carver to see it any other way. Unless he begins believing in the supernatural. And where will that lead him? Maybe then he'll be the one murdering people.

No, there had to be another explanation. Some people buckled under the stress of living and went off the rails at the most unusual times. But a triple homicide? What would he gain from such cruelty?

Stress relief was all Carver could come up with, but he knew that wasn't accurate. It all seemed just too…

Clean.

For lack of a better word. As if Jerry was sent over the rails to cover the evil that existed beneath the folds. A scapegoat who lost his mind, allowing the public to point their bony fingers and cluck their tongues as they suggest so delicately to lock up the terrible and evil Jerry Hardwood. So they can feel safe and put their fears to rest for at least one night. As if there wasn't another devil waiting in the shadows to leap at them and claw their hearts out.

So, the true evil can have time to gain strength before beginning again.

The revelation struck Carver like a bullet through his head.

Put the present to bed, he told himself. Learn from it and use the information to see the signs when they return. Only then will he be able to put this situation to rest once and for all. Carver snapped the pencil he'd been squeezing in his hands.

A sudden cringe rifled through his bones. He saw what he'd written across his report. In thick black letters, the words stared at him:

Initium Novum!

53

Two days later, Lori was discharged from the hospital. Having ran every test imaginable, the doctors declared a genuine miracle with Lori's condition. There were no adverse effects. None whatsoever. It was as if her wounds had never existed.

No injuries except for the heart, which was not just broken but shattered into a million pieces, as if Marc had taken a baseball bat and swung for the fences, exploding her fragile heart. She felt hollow inside, as if that shattered heart was replaced by a void that could never be filled or repaired.

Lori felt like everything was in slow motion, as if she couldn't do one single thing without the impression of pain impinging on her bones, weighing her down into a depression unlike any she'd ever experienced. Even as they wheeled her out of the hospital-standard protocol was to use a wheelchair for any patient who'd sustained a head injury, despite if said injury were healed prior to release-she couldn't help but think back to the letter and how it crushed every ounce of strength she ever had.

At first, she remained skeptical. Although the handwriting was a spot on match, she held onto the possibility that someone else had written the letter. But the nurse, Jessica, confirmed that Marc was the author and that he came to the unit to see her before returning home.

Home. That word took on a new meaning now that Marc was gone. Sleepy Hollow had become her home, the place where she earned her independence, her much needed independence, and a place where she could allow herself to grow and evolve into the person she liked to see in the mirror in the morning. A place where she could prosper in her own way and define success by her terms and not by societal norms of power, money, control, and stately homes large enough to prove the existence of power belonged to the one who owned that home. A place where she could find true love and run away with it, far away from the life she despised more than any-the life her parents had made for her.

Marc's letter shed little light on the reasons he ended the engagement. She always knew he was unstable, but that was the part of Marc she found intriguing.

Disturbed is how she first described him. Brilliant and disturbed. But also, passionate and courteous beneath the veneer. Gentle. She knew he had difficulty coping with death, although she would never have guessed he would run away so quickly. Not from her, at least. Not ever from her. Perhaps the thought of losing her, the fact that life was so fragile and could be gone in a blink, left him debilitated with fear and he believed he had to let her go. Or maybe, just maybe, he saw Lori's condition and freaked out, not wanting to face the possibility that Lori would perish. Perhaps he wanted to keep her in his memory as she was because it was easier to let go than to face death head on.

There was enough death in his life already.

Lori watched as the black SUV pulled in front of her by the curb. Her mother was in the back seat and normally Lori would have cringed when she laid eyes on her, but not today. Today she was numb to her core, moving mechanically through the moment. Doing what she was told without question. Not that it mattered. Not that any of it mattered one iota now that Marc was gone. The nurse who wheeled her from the hospital offered his hand, but Lori waved him off-she didn't need a helping hand. What she knew was that she didn't want to climb into the SUV. She wanted to go home. Home to Sleepy Hollow. Her home. Not the one where her mother stood center stage, barking orders. Lori stared at the SUV as if she were staring at the door to hell.

Elena climbed out after the driver opened her door. "Are you ready?"

Lori cleared her throat and nodded as she pushed herself off the wheelchair. "I need to gather my things from my apartment." Lori eyeballed her mother, wanting nothing more than a chance to see Marc. To stare into his eyes and let him tell her he no longer wanted her. Maybe then she could put the present into the past and move on.

Elena stood tall, raising her chin. "I already gathered everything from your apartment. It's all at home. You can go through everything when we arrive." Her eyes narrowed, staring at Lori. "Come," she said, "We have a long drive, and I'd like to be home before sunset." Elena turned and climbed back into the SUV.

Lori paused. Leave it to Elena to take control of the situation, a manner that Lori had grown accustomed to. She should have anticipated such an action. She turned to the sky and felt how cold the air had grown. Autumn's chill had arrived early and came with a vengeance.

Storms comin, she heard Marc's voice. Her last memory before the world went dark. The last words she remembered Marc ever saying were when they climbed into that steel coffin and drove into the storm. The chill rippled across her skin, and she crossed her arms to ward it off.

The storm is definitely coming.

Lori climbed into the SUV, the door closed by the driver, who then walked around to the driver's seat.

Lori shifted in her seat. "I still want to go home," she said and cleared her throat. "To make sure you got everything." Reluctantly, she looked at her mother, and the narrowed glare beaming from Elena's eyes.

"No, you want to track down Marc. I know you, Lori, and what you want is not good."

Lori turned to the window as the driver shifted into drive and the SUV hummed through the parking lot towards the exit. Her eyes filled with tears. "Why can't I just go home?"

"I didn't do this, Lori. I didn't cause the accident, and I definitely did not write that letter. He did, and I'm sorry for what you're going through, but we both know what happened the last time you had a broken heart, and I'll be damned before I allow you to do the same. Plus, the doctor said to monitor for adverse effects. You'll need someone to stay with you for a while. This is all for the best."

Lori looked down at her trembling hands, her tears cascaded to her jawline. She looked up. Looked out the window, staring mindlessly.

She didn't say another word during the long trip home to the Hamptons. Every mile the SUV clawed across was like a further stretch into hell, with thoughts rattling through her brain that were filled with desperation, despair, and wretchedness. Lori remembered too what happened the last time her heart was broken. She swallowed a bottle of pills.

And at this moment, she wished she had succeeded in her endeavor. The anguish she was going through was too much to bear.

54

Marc was drifting in the darkness. Floating, wandering endlessly, screaming and petrified.

Those teeth. The presence in the mausoleum had come through him and kept him in the darkness. He couldn't find his way back to the cemetery. Couldn't find the door he had ripped open in a fever filled with fear. He'd become alone in the darkness, alone but with the teeth overseeing him. Watching his every move.

The darkness was an endless void that swallowed him whole. As if inside the mausoleum there existed a new world-a world within and in-between our own-and this other world birthed demons and devils with the purpose of torturing the dead. But even as he ran, walked, and huffed, he could feel the malevolent presence, on his heels, in front of him, always with him, like a guard belonging to the darkness and it was everywhere. Following him and keeping him in the darkness. He ran until he couldn't run any longer, his legs throbbing with an ache that stiffened his limbs.

Marc had a feeling that if he continued to run, he'd wake up in a hell more dire than the darkness. As if something existed beyond the darkness that was waiting for him like a cannibal licking its chops in the presence of fresh meat. As if he was being hunted. And the hunter enjoyed toying with its prey.

Quiet consumed him. As if that quiet were its own entity, watching him, escorting him beyond the darkness. To the place where Marc feared to travel. He stopped and bent over, holding his aching legs. His breath caught in his chest. Watching, staring, looking at the ground when there was no ground, just a speed traveling fog that raced through his legs towards the beyond. The fog that crackled every so often with a bluish spark like electricity.

Now he could see an outline of trees up ahead, dark and foreboding, with bare limbs that sat dead and in waiting. Trees, thick and tall, shone in the darkness as if those trees existed inside the dark, submerged in an ocean of black and faded into the fabric of pitch. Felt how cold the air had grown as if hell existed not in a burning fire but in the stinging cold of eternal winter. His skin frozen and burning from the wind's icy breath.

Marc peered into the darkness, looking past the trees into the shadows existing between trunks and roots and branches and twigs. Shadows with eyes born from fear and unknowing death.

A branch snapped behind him, and he turned on his heels to the sound. Nothing. His breath huffed from his throat. His chest heaved with a thick gasp. He pursed his lips and swallowed. Then quiet, as Marc attempted to listen, to hear the mumbles and grumbles from the dead. He looked up, looked up high, but there was no sky, no moon to light the night. Just bare trees reaching into darkness.

Another twig snapped, only this time when he turned, he saw the apparition between the trees. But not just one, many, as if they'd surrounded him. Some were bent over on all fours, standing like proud wolves ready to devour their surrounded prey. Their eyes gleamed red, and their ivory fangs were stained with blood. Marc's heart thundered in his chest, his breath stuttering in his throat, across his trembling lips. His eyes darted from left to right. So many malicious ghosts, so many souls' hell bent on revenge and suffering.

They were everywhere. Creeping towards him like flickers of electricity. Marc spiraled around, looking for a safe venue to run to but there was no such luck and no escape as they crept towards him. And with every flicker, they drew closer. The ghosts of the western woods. He knew it was them.

"Help me," Marc groaned, but who he was groaning to he did not know. Gritting his teeth in preparation for the dead, he felt a hand, wet and slick brush across the nape of his neck and he spun around.

"Initium Novum!" The voice was rickety, like a cackle from the throat of the old that boomed across the firmament. It was followed by a bellowing laugh that echoed across the sky. A high-pitched cackle that vibrated in his bones. "Every beginning has an end."

Marc watched as the woman materialized inside the fog-drenched atmosphere. Her red eyes came first, followed by her face, hair, shoulders, then body. Her skin, so soft and fair, carried the essence of youth. Long dark hair cascaded to her shoulders where a black cloak draped down to her ankles, tied around the waist by a green rope. Her eyes were wide as if in anticipation, her lips parted, nose curled in a forever snarl. She moved as if she was a part of the wind, her body contorting and flickering as she walked, talking in tongues, whispered from a hoarse throat.

Marc backed up as she drew closer, words flitting off her lips in rapid succession. All he could see were her eyes as she glided closer. He could feel her breath on his skin, and it cringed his bones. It seemed like she was floating towards him, her toes scraping across the earth. He backed up some more, stumbled and dropped onto his ass.

"What do you want from me?" Marc's words stuttered across his lips.

She gripped his forehead, continuing to speak in tongues when she said, "Just your heart, Marc Saduj." And she thrust her fist into his chest and squeezed his heart. Marc felt an immediate freeze in his bones as pain tore through his chest. He looked down and saw that her hand had passed effortlessly through his body. She was squeezing his heart. He couldn't breathe, suffocating on pain and fear.

She dipped her head closer to his. "I need hearts for the master." Her voice was raspy, sinister, then she vanished into thin air. A thin whisp of fog floated in front of him, then faded. Dark black night replaced her existence. Marc looked inside the darkness, his eyes flitting from one ghost to the other. Heard the woman cackle her laugh across the cemetery.

The ghosts were on top of him then. Blood-red eyes and sharp teeth surrounded him, and Marc screamed. Screamed because there was nothing left for him to do as they rushed at him, and Marc felt himself fall. Falling with that scream bellowing from his throat. Fell with his eyes closed until he landed with a squeak.

Marc snapped his eyes open to the daylight that washed through his window. Heard a hum coming from outside, along with voices and laughter as he looked around when relief washed over him. He was in his bedroom in his apartment. The sounds were coming from outside, through the open window. And the vision from his slumber raced into oblivion. He sat up, trying to connect his thoughts as the wind billowed through the open window, cold and crisp, and he heard a click followed by voices in his living room.

Marc shot up, staring into the hallway, stiff with his breath caught in his throat. The voices beamed from the living room. There were two voices, a man and woman, then laughter. He bent his head, listening, when he realized the voices were coming from his television.

Did he leave it on? Marc couldn't connect his thoughts to the time. Where had he been? How long had he been asleep? Another icy breeze raced through his window, rippling across his skin. He went to step towards the hallway when his foot came off the hardwood floor with a wet squelch.

His sneakers were caked in a dark, wet sludge. The same sludge he found on his bed sheets. And he felt off, unbalanced, his hands trembling and he felt sick, as if his blood had been infected with poison turning his stomach into a noxious cesspool of gas and nausea.

"I've got to stop drinking," he whispered, squeezing his feet out of his sneakers. His head heavy and weary, he went into the living room and low and behold the television was on, blaring the local news with the weatherman laughing with his anchor.

Marc stared at the television, confused. All his windows were open, the cold rippling through his apartment. He must have left the television on and opened all the windows in a drunken haze before he passed out.

But where did that sludge come from?

He thought and thought, remembering the storm.

Must have gone outside. But why?

I don't know.

Felt puke in the back of his throat. He closed his eyes, trying to remember, but with no such luck and when he opened his eyes, he noticed the empty bottle of Scotch next to an empty glass on the side table beside his chair. The bottle stood by the phone with the nurse Jessica's card next to it.

Lori?

He took his seat, grabbed the receiver, and dialed Jessica's number, then sat back, listening to the ring, staring at the newscast, waiting, and hoping she would answer.

How long had he been asleep? He hoped he didn't miss a potential phone call with an update on Lori's condition. He studied the newscast, his stare drifting to the bottom right corner when he craned his head, and his eyes narrowed. On the screen he could see the temperature-54 degrees-with a sun and cloud behind it, and below the temperature was the date-September 5th.

Can't be.

The phone rang in his ear.

That would mean I've been sleeping for three days.

Nothing's adding up.

The phone call was answered with a resounding and hurried, "Hello, ICU unit."

Marc jumped up in his chair. "Hello, Jessica? It's Marc… Marc Saduj. I wanted to see how Lori Francon is doing?"

The pause seemed to last a lifetime, and when she talked, her voice was a whisper, a stern whisper, but a whisper no less. "Marc, I tried calling you several times." Another pause but Marc had no response. He had no idea what was going on. "Lori was discharged yesterday."

Now he perked up. *Discharged?* "How is that possible?"

"Miraculous recovery. Her last surgery was a success."

Yesterday? "Where did she discharge to?"

"Home with her mother."

Her mother?

His scar started itching, burning. He pressed against it and his vision blurred. *Why would Lori return home with her mother?*

None of this made any sense.

"Are you certain about that? Lori and her mother don't…"

"I'm certain." Another pause. "She said she was going to write you a letter explaining her decision." Marc squeezed the receiver, listening to it creak as he pressed against his throbbing scar. "I'm sure she did. She was very adamant about explaining things to you. Did you get the letter?"

Marc paused before he said, "No," then dropped the receiver on its cradle.

Letter? Lori wrote him a letter explaining the situation. He shot up from his seat, the newscast still blaring today's most prominent news stories, but he couldn't take his eyes off the date.

Did Lori try to call him? Maybe she had no other option and had to go home with Elena? No other option because Marc was passed out drunk and obviously got into some really strange shit, considering the sludge on his sneakers.

Letter?

He stomped into the kitchen to retrieve his mailbox key when he saw it. The letter Jessica was referring to was on his table next to another empty bottle of Scotch. He stared at that letter as if it were the devil himself. Quite obvious he'd read it already. Read it and went on a drunken spree of depression while swimming in alcohol. There was an envelope beneath the letter but there was no stamp on the envelope. Just a clean white envelope. No name. No stamp. Nothing.

Was she here? Did she talk to him or just drop off the letter?

He couldn't find the memory, or any memory of the last three days, as if there were holes in his brain, dark caverns that reached into oblivion that swallowed his memories.

Maybe someone's fucking with me?

He sat down to assess the handwriting. He could tell Lori's handwriting as if it were his own. Marc had seen her write a thousand times and he was certain she had written what was on the page. He scanned the letter, reading words like, *I'm sorry, it's for the best*, and *I can't continue like this. We're not good for each other.* His hand trembled as tears filled his eyes when his heart shattered, reading what Lori had written. *I shouldn't have said yes.*

He sat on that chair until the sun descended on Sleepy Hollow, twirling the dark green rope around his wrist. Mindlessly, as if the rope had always been there. As if it were a part of him that he could never take off. In his mind, he always had the rope around his wrist. It represented connection. Connection to something larger than himself. A connection he could never understand. Marc stared mindlessly through his window for what seemed like an eternity, at first in denial and then into madness. Hate and rage pierced his heart like a knife.

It was over. The how and the why behind the decision did not matter. It was over. Gone. Done.

I shouldn't have said yes.

A void erupted in his gut, in his heart too. A hollowed-out void filled with agony.

He sat until darkness filled his apartment, and the icy wind took a permanent space in his heart. Sat with thoughts speeding through his brain, numb to his core. Sat until the early morning twilight arrived with an even colder chill.

Sat until he heard the knock on his door. The rapping called him to it.

Marc understood he had to answer the door. In the dark recesses of his mind, he knew he had a debt to repay.

Even if he didn't understand why.

Also by PD Alleva

Horror

Golem: A haunting tale of suspense, loss, isolation, contempt, and fear. The Devil is in the details!

Jigglyspot and the Zero Intellect: A satirical cosmic horror fantasy thriller novel. Jigglyspot is a half-human, half-warlock, travelling carnival clown moonlighting as a drug dealing pimp and lackey for a demonic army from Xibalba.

Sci-Fi/Fantasy

The Dark Veil: The Rose Vol 1 & 2: A masterful, dystopian science fiction thriller of telepathic evil greys, mysterious rebellion, martial arts, and Alien Vampires.

Dark Fantasy

Presenting the Marriage of Kelli Anne & Gerri Denemer: One known terrorist. A protest about to erupt. A family on the brink of collapse. Is the bond between husband and wife strong enough to defeat evil?

Purchase these and other fine books of horror, scifi, and psychological thrillers from the author at **pdalleva.com**

PD's Alternative Fiction publishes weekly serialized fiction stories in the horror, scifi, and psychological thriller genres. Subscribe at pdalleva.com and receive a FREE digital copy of PD's latest cosmic release, "Election Retrograde."

About the Author

PD writes books. Horror, scifi, psychological thrillers, fantasy, and sometimes a literary gem. Good ones, crazy ones, fun books, entertaining books, terrifying books that are absolutely insane, and books with depth and thrills that rip out the heart of humanity then tosses it on a slab to be feasted on. Yeah, that's what he does, he writes books. Any questions?

To learn more or join PD's newsletter visit pdalleva.com.

www.ingramcontent.com/pod-product-compliance
Lightning Source LLC
Chambersburg PA
CBHW030130010826

48973CB00002B/496